THE KINGFISHER
TREASURY of STORIES for CHILDREN

Nancy & Edward Blishen

Kingfisher Books, Grisewood & Dempsey Ltd,
Elsley House, 24–30 Great Titchfield Street, London W1P 7AD

First published in 1992 by Kingfisher Books
2 4 6 8 10 9 7 5 3 1

Material in this edition was previously published in
A Treasury of Stories for Five Year Olds (1989), *A Treasury
of Stories for Six Year Olds* (1988) and *A Treasury of Stories
for Seven Year Olds* (1988).

BRITISH LIBRARY CATALOGUING IN PUBLICATION DATA
A catalogue record for this book is available from the British Library

ISBN 0 86272 923 8
Printed and bound in Slovenia by Ljudska Pravica

THE KINGFISHER
TREASURY
of STORIES *for*
CHILDREN

Chosen by
NANCY AND EDWARD BLISHEN

Illustrated by
PATRICIA LUDLOW, TIZZIE KNOWLES
AND POLLY NOAKES

Kingfisher Books

CONTENTS

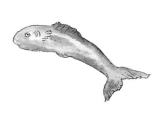

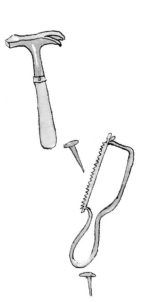
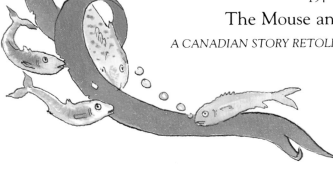

JOHNNY-CAKE

Joseph Jacobs

Once upon a time there was an old man, and an old woman, and a little boy. One morning the old woman made a Johnny-cake, and put it in the oven to bake. "You watch the Johnny-cake while your father and I go out to work in the garden." So the old man and the old woman went out and began to hoe potatoes, and left the little boy to tend the oven. But he didn't watch it all the time, and all of a sudden he heard a noise, and he looked up and the oven door popped open, and out of the oven jumped Johnny-cake, and went rolling along end over end, towards the open door of the house. The little boy ran to shut the door, but Johnny-cake was too quick for him and rolled through the door, down the steps, and out into the road long before the little boy could catch him. The little boy ran after him as fast as he could clip it, crying out to his father and mother, who heard the uproar, and threw down their hoes and gave chase too. But Johnny-cake outran all three a long way, and was soon out of sight, while they had to sit down, all out of breath, on a bank to rest.

On went Johnny-cake, and by and by he came to two well-diggers who looked up from their work and called out: "Where ye going, Johnny-cake?"

He said: "I've outrun an old man, and an old woman, and a little boy, and I can outrun you, too-o-o!"

"Ye can, can ye? We'll see about that!" said they; and they threw down their picks and ran after him, but couldn't catch up with him, and soon they had to sit down by the roadside to rest.

On ran Johnny-cake, and by and by he came to two ditch-diggers who were digging a ditch. "Where ye going, Johnny-cake?" said they. He said: "I've outrun an old man, and an old woman, and a little boy, and two well-diggers, and I can outrun you, too-o-o!"

"Ye can, can ye? We'll see about that!" said they; and they threw down their spades, and ran after him too. But Johnny-cake soon outstripped them also, and seeing they could never catch him, they gave up the chase and sat down to rest.

On went Johnny-cake, and by and by he came to a bear. The bear said: "Where are ye going, Johnny-cake?"

He said: "I've outrun an old man, and an old woman, and a little boy, and two well-diggers, and two ditch-diggers, and I can outrun you, too-o-o!"

"Ye can, can ye?" growled the bear. "We'll see about that!" and trotted as fast as his legs could carry him after Johnny-cake, who never stopped to look behind him. Before long the bear was left so far behind that he saw he might as well give up the hunt first as last, so he stretched himself out by the roadside to rest.

On went Johnny-cake, and by and by he came to a wolf. The wolf said: "Where ye going, Johnny-cake?"

He said: "I've outrun an old man, and an old woman, and a little boy, and two well-diggers, and two ditch-diggers, and a bear, and I can outrun you, too-o-o!"

"Ye can, can ye?" snarled the wolf. "We'll see about that!" And he set into a gallop after Johnny-cake, who went on and on so fast that the wolf, too, saw there was no hope of overtaking him, and he, too, lay down to rest.

On went Johnny-cake, and by and by he came to a fox that lay quietly in a corner of the fence. The fox called out in a sharp voice, but without getting up: "Where ye going, Johnny-cake?"

He said: "I've outrun an old man, and an old woman,

and a little boy, and two well-diggers, and two ditch-diggers, a bear, and a wolf, and I can outrun you, too-o-o!"

The fox said: "I can't quite hear you, Johnny-cake; won't you come a little closer?" and he turned his head a little to one side.

Johnny-cake stopped his race for the first time, and went a little closer, and called out in a very loud voice: "*I've outrun an old man, and an old woman, and a little boy, and two well-diggers, and two ditch-diggers, and a bear, and a wolf, and I can outrun you, too-o-o.*"

"Can't quite hear you; won't you come a *little* closer?" said the fox in a feeble voice, as he stretched out his neck towards Johnny-cake, and put one paw behind his ear.

Johnny-cake came up close, and leaning towards the fox screamed out: "I'VE OUTRUN AN OLD MAN, AND AN OLD WOMAN, AND A LITTLE BOY, AND TWO WELL-DIGGERS, AND TWO DITCH-DIGGERS, AND A BEAR, AND A WOLF, AND I CAN OUTRUN YOU, TOO-O-O!"

"You can, can you?" yelped the fox, and snapped up the Johnny-cake in his sharp teeth in the twinkling of an eye.

THE WITCH AND THE LITTLE VILLAGE BUS

Margaret Stuart Barry

Simon was late for school. So that was how he came to jump on the village bus. And that was how he happened to meet Ginny the witch. He had sat down next to her before he had properly noticed her.

She was a very ugly old witch. She had a pale green face, tiny red eyes like hot cinders, a spot on the end of her long nose, and grey hair which reached down to her knees. Simon was pleased. He liked witches. He hoped she was going to be a really wicked old witch like the ones he had read about.

"What have you got in your bag?" he asked her.

"In my bag? – My magic wand, of course, my Post Office Savings Book, and my knitting."

"Oh," said Simon.

He was a little disappointed. He had hoped that the witch would have had a black toad, or at least a couple of dead spiders. They were passing the school gates, but Simon was too interested to notice.

"Fares please," said the conductor. Simon paid his fare.

"Fares," said the conductor to the witch.

"You forgot to say 'please'," reminded Ginny the witch.

"Why should I say 'please' to an old witch like you," said the conductor, rudely.

"Because it's manners," replied the witch.

"Fares!" snapped the conductor.

"If you do not say 'please', I shall change your silly old bus into something else."

The conductor was now very cross. "Shan't," he said.

At that, the witch opened her handbag and started to search for her wand. As soon as she found it, she changed the bus into a fast express train.

"Wheeeeeee!" went the fast express train. It shot down the village street, through the red lights, and out on to the motorway. On the motorway was a big sign which said – LONDON 50 MILES.

"Hey!" shouted Farmer Spud. "I do not want to go to London. I want to go to Little Hampton to buy a pig."

"Hey!" shouted Mrs Gummidge. "I do not want to go to London either. I want to go to Little Hampton to buy some shoelaces."

"Hey!" said the bus driver. "I do not know how to drive this thing. It is much too fast."

Ginny the witch said nothing. She took her knitting out of her bag and began to knit, very fast. Simon was delighted.

It was not very long before the roaring train reached London. There were cars and buses everywhere. The train was bumping into them one after another.

"This is terrible!" said the conductor. "Stop, stop it!"

"I will if you say 'please'. Otherwise I shall change your silly old train into something else."

"I will not say 'please' to a witch," shouted the rude conductor.

"Suit yourself," said Ginny. She put away her knitting, searched again for her wand, and changed the train into a green caterpillar.

"Help!" cried Farmer Spud, falling off.

"Help!" cried Mrs Gummidge, falling off also.

"Help! Help!" cried the conductor and the bus driver.

The caterpillar was far too slippery to ride on. It was also much too small. The passengers were obliged to walk alongside it.

"This is ridiculous!" complained Farmer Spud. "I have never been on a bus like this in the whole of my life."

"You are not on it man, are you!" snapped Mrs Gummidge, irritably.

"Watch it!" cried the bus driver. "It's going down that grid!"

Laughing, Simon rescued the little caterpillar and set it on its way again. It was actually a great deal of trouble and bother watching the caterpillar. First it went this way, and then the other. It did not seem to have any clear idea where it wanted to go. The bus driver was extremely worried about it. He had to get his bus back to the Depot by six o'clock. It was already half past four. Suddenly a big policeman stepped into the road to direct the traffic.

"Watch out!" gasped the bus driver. "You're stepping on our bus!"

The big London policeman looked around in all directions. He could not see a bus. He could see only a bus driver, a conductor, a farmer, an old woman, a small boy, and a very ugly witch.

"I'm busy," he said. "Mind out."

"This is terrible," moaned the bus driver. "For goodness sake, say 'please' to the old witch."

"I cannot possibly," said the conductor. "I never say 'please' to witches."

"Suit yourself," said Ginny. She had almost finished her knitting.

It was nearing the Rush Hour. The Rush Hour is a terrible thing. Trains and buses and cars and people rush about everywhere in a great hurry. They squash and push and squeeze each other. There is certainly no room for a caravan drawn by six cart-horses. So this is what the witch decided to do. She pulled out her wand and changed the little caterpillar into a handsome caravan, drawn by six cart-horses. The caravan took up a lot more room than the caterpillar had done. Moreover, the cart-horses could not tell green lights from red lights: they clattered clumsily on. They did not understand what the policemen were shouting about. When cars and buses kicked them, they kicked back with a will.

"This is great!" cried Simon. "It's better than school!"

"This is monstrous!" cried the bus driver.

"My pig! My shoelaces!" cried Farmer Spud and Mrs Gummidge together, looking at the time. It was now five o'clock. They would never get back to the Depot. The six cart-horses caught sight of Hyde Park. It looked nice and green. They trotted in for a feed of grass.

"They can't do that!" exclaimed the bus driver. "There isn't time!"

"It's your conductor who is making us late – not my horses," said Ginny. "Anyway, I'm tired." She hung up her hat on a branch and sat down under a tree for a nap.

"She's going to sleep!" cried Farmer Spud, indignantly. He shook her, and said, "Wake up, wake up – you bad old witch."

"Go away," yawned Ginny. "I've had a hard day."

No one knew what to do – except Simon. He had run off to play with the horses. He did not mind one bit how late it was.

Then Mrs Gummidge got very cross. "Now just you listen to me, conductor," she scolded – prodding him in the tummy with her umbrella. "It is high time we went home. We have had enough of this nonsense. Mend your manners and say 'please' to that old witch at once."

"But I never say 'please' to . . ."

Mrs Gummidge poked her umbrella a little harder.

"Oh, very well," grumbled the conductor. He was worn out anyway. He shuffled over to Ginny.

"Fares please," he said in a sulky voice.

Ginny opened one red eye, and said, "Pardon?"

"Fares please," said the conductor again.

Ginny put one finger into her ear and rubbed it very hard until it squeaked. "Pardon?" she said again.

"Fares – please." This time the conductor said it very politely.

"Now that's better!" declared the witch.

She whisked out her wand and she changed the caravan and the six cart-horses into a big jet. Everybody scrambled in as fast as they could.

"Zooooom!" went the jet – and before the bus driver, or the conductor, or the farmer, or the old woman, or the little boy had time to think – they were in Little Hampton.

The shops were shut, so it was too late for Farmer Spud to buy his pig, or Mrs Gummidge her shoelaces. But it was still only one minute before six o'clock – just enough time for the witch to change the big jet plane back into the village bus.

"Thank you, Madam," said the conductor – very politely.

"You're welcome," said the witch. "Any time."

Then she went home with Simon, to explain to Simon's mother why he was home a little late for tea.

BEAUTIFUL CATHARINELLA

The Brothers Grimm

Long long ago, in a village in Italy, lived a man and his wife who had a daughter called Catharinella. She had such lovely fair hair that words cannot describe how beautiful were the plaits wound round her head.

The father was a soldier, and just when a new baby was to be born he was called away to the wars. At that time the mother was always hungry for parsley, and soon had eaten up all there was in her garden. Next she went the round of her neighbours' gardens, till at length there wasn't the tiniest sprig of parsley left in the whole village. The only bit remaining near grew in the garden of an ogre who lived in a great palace outside the village.

The poor woman wept and was very unhappy because she feared that she and her unborn child would die of starvation. Seeing the sad state her dear mother was in, Catharinella too was sad, and at last decided to go every day and steal as much parsley from the ogre's garden as her mother wanted. When the ogre went round each night to see how his garden grew, he found the parsley plants getting fewer and fewer; and he shook his head angrily, while his long beard swept the box-hedge lining the beds on both sides. As this did not seem to mend matters much, he at last strewed ashes secretly along the path.

So in the morning, when Catharinella went as usual to fetch her mother's parsley, the ashes stuck to her little slippers, and the ogre easily traced the way to her cottage. He followed her in, and appearing to be very angry he threatened that unless she came to the palace as his servant he would eat her. The poor mother sobbed bitterly, not wanting the girl to go; but when the ogre promised that no harm would come to her – he would even let her pick each day all the parsley her mother wanted – it was agreed, and Catharinella departed with her new master.

Now the ogre was not really as fierce and wicked as he looked, but just a little lazy; and when he came home in the evening after eating heartily he hated to climb the stairs. So he shouted from below the window, "Catharinella, Catharinella, let your golden plaits down and lift me into the house," and the girl did so; and that was all the work she had to do. She enjoyed an easy life, with plenty to eat and drink; and she had lots of fun talking to the furniture, for it was enchanted.

As he got older, the ogre grew lazier and lazier, till he didn't want to do a thing for himself, and even took in a young man to help with the magic. This was a smart, nice-looking fellow, who had not got a long beard, nor did he wait long at the door when *he* wished to see Catharinella – no, he leapt up the stairs drawn by the beautiful golden plaits in quite a different way from the ogre! Every day the ogre seemed heavier and heavier to the girl, and she disliked him so much that she was well pleased when the young wizard offered to conjure up a coach and horses to take them away.

Soon everything was ready for their flight, but as all the pieces of furniture could talk the pair were afraid they might blab and the old ogre would learn where they had gone — and before they were far enough off for him not to catch up with them. So they thought and they thought what they could do to keep the furniture quiet. In the end Catharinella decided she would cook a great potful of macaroni and treat them, lock, stock and barrel, to this tasty dish. She soon set to work, and when the macaroni was cooked she stood the great pot in the main hall and invited everything in the house to eat its fill. It must have been a funny sight indeed to see chairs, settles, tables and all, come running! — mirrors and pictures flying down off the walls; stout old cupboards stumbling along; china sets and glasses tripping lightly — all to enjoy the treat. They made a dreadful din, all the big and little mouths busily munching, and even the great pot itself now and again gulping down some of its own contents. When they had eaten all they could, they promised to say nothing that would betray the kind folk who had fed them. And in fact all would have been well, if an old besom in a corner of the attic had not been forgotten. He went stumping round the house in a rage, shouting all the time, "They've all eaten macaroni — but they've forgotten me!" In vain Catharinella tried to soothe him down, but there was nothing she could do save get away as quickly as possible with her young man. This she did, not taking a thing with her but a brush, a comb and a mirror, to keep her hair tidy.

That night, when the ogre came home, he shouted as usual, "Catharinella, Catharinella, let your golden plaits down and lift me into the house." But there was no answer. When at last he grew impatient and forced the door, the

old besom came to meet him, all tousle-haired and excited, struggling to pour out everything; but as he had said nothing else all day, he could only repeat "They've all eaten macaroni – but they've forgotten me!" The ogre grasped that something was wrong, and went round asking the other household things to tell, but all were so stuffed with food that they gave nothing away. Yet he soon got an idea of what had happened.

He tucked up his cloak, tied three knots in his long beard – so that it couldn't get in his way in running – and took up the chase. In a short time he sighted the pair in the distance, in the magic coach. Nearer and nearer he drew, till he could reach out for Catharinella, who was just looking out of the coach window. In her panic she flung her comb at him – and in a trice it changed into iron bars, which caught the ogre's beard as he tried to get across. In the end he succeeded and almost clutched the coach; but now Catharinella flung out her brush, which instantly turned into a thorn-bush. The ogre's beard got caught again, and his cloak torn; but once more he managed to struggle through and come near the coach. Then Catharinella threw out the mirror.

It turned into a lake, and drowned the ogre.

THE TOYMAKER'S SHOP

Marie Smith

The shop with the bright yellow door and shiny doorknob was tucked away at the end of a very small street, next to a sweet shop. It had a swinging sign that said THE TOYMAKER'S SHOP.

The Toymaker had lived there for many years. He was famous for making the most beautiful toys. But he broke his glasses; and because he could barely see without them, there was now something wrong with all the toys he made. None of the boys and girls who came into his shop bought anything. Soon they stopped coming altogether, and the bright yellow door remained closed.

Well, for example, the Toymaker had painted the dolls' faces a powdery blue. He had made a grandfather clock that went tock, tock, tock, but never tick, and soldiers that marched around the room backwards. There was a rag doll wearing only one pink shoe, and a dancing doll with no shoes at all. Sinbad the Sailor had two wooden legs, instead of only one. As for the King and Queen puppets, they didn't look like a King and Queen at all except for their crowns made from yellow glass beads. Humpty Dumpty was an egg, all right, but he had a long hairy tail. Clancy the

25

Clown looked too cross to be a clown, and he was sitting in long skinny Jack's box. So Jack-in-the-box was Jack-out-of-the-box, and had to sit on a window-sill.

But the worst mistake of all had been made with Merlin the Wizard. He should have had a wand in his hand, but instead he was carrying a china-blue egg. What's more, his starry hat kept slipping over his eyes.

One night the King decided he could bear it no longer. The little yellow door hadn't opened for weeks. So he called the toys together, cleared his royal throat and said:

"Something really *must* be done! We simply can't go on looking like this!" He looked down at his gown. It should have been purple and splendid, but instead it was ragged and grey.

"Do you remember," said the King, "the silver fairy the Toymaker made before he broke his glasses? He made a wand for her. Someone bought her, but when the Toymaker wrapped her up, she dropped her wand. And he couldn't find it. Do you remember?"

The toys nodded and the King continued.

"It must be here somewhere. Now, if we could find it, the Wizard might be able to do

26

magic with it and make us look as we ought to look."

At once they all began to hunt for the wand. They looked in boxes, big and small. They looked under the stairs. They lifted up the rugs and looked under them. They looked in a tiny yellow teapot that the Toymaker had made with two spouts and no handle. They looked in a big brown jug that had two handles and no spout.

They looked everywhere, but the wand was nowhere to be seen.

The King gave a huge royal sigh.

"If we don't want to stay as we are for ever, we must go on looking," he said. And he took out his royal handkerchief (which the Toymaker had made far too small), mopped his royal brow and sat down next to Sinbad the Sailor.

Now, Sinbad was fast asleep, and he hadn't actually done any looking. To make himself comfortable he'd unscrewed one of his hollow wooden legs and given it to a blue-faced doll to hold for him. Then he'd begun to snore.

That made the King angry, and he tried to take the leg from the doll. Let Sinbad put it on and go looking for the wand like everyone else! But the doll, who was rather afraid of Sinbad, held on to it. And as she struggled with the King, the leg broke in half.

And out of it fell a long, slender stick.

"*There* it is!" cried the King. "It's the wand! It was inside Sinbad's leg!"

The wand shone and glowed, and the King picked it up and gave it to Merlin. The Wizard dropped the china-blue egg, pushed up his hat so he could see what he was doing, stroked his long white beard and touched the King on the head with the wand.

There was a loud bang and a cloud of smoke. And when the smoke had cleared away, every toy had turned into a wooden clothes-peg.

"Great Scott!" cried the Wizard. "What *have* I done?" He looked unhappily at the King who, like the rest, was now a plain dull wooden peg. "I must try again!"

Another explosion. More smoke. And now the toys had become green, hairy *hats*.

In despair Merlin stroked his long white beard twice before waving the wand again. By chance the tip of the wand touched one of the stars on his hat.

There was an enormous bang and another great cloud of smoke. And this time, those awful green hairy hats had turned back into toys. Yet how different they looked! They had become as beautiful and well-made as they should have been.

The King, wearing robes of purple and a golden crown, said to the Wizard,

"Now you know how to use the wand, we must mend the Toymaker's glasses. *At once!*"

They crept up the stairs to the Toymaker's bedroom. His old broken glasses lay on a table beside the bed. The Wizard touched them with his wand, and they became bright and new. Then they crept downstairs again and looked at one another with great satisfaction.

For Sinbad the Sailor now had only one wooden leg. The Wizard's hat stayed on his head. The rag doll and the dancing doll had new shoes. The toy soldiers marched smartly round the room forwards. The dolls' faces had turned pink; and as for the Clown, he had the sort of face a clown ought to have, round and laughing. Long skinny Jack was back in the box where he belonged, and Humpty Dumpty had lost his tail.

As for the grandfather clock going tock, tock, tock for so long, it was now going tick, tock, tick, tock, tick, tock . . .

And the little yellow door was preparing itself for the next day. It knew that when the children looked through the window and saw how beautiful the toys were, they'd be turning the shiny doorknob and pouring into the Toymaker's shop.

THE LITTLE BOY
WHO DIDN'T ALWAYS
TELL THE TRUTH
A traditional French tale

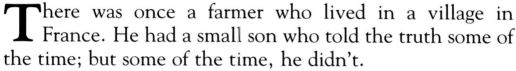

There was once a farmer who lived in a village in France. He had a small son who told the truth some of the time; but some of the time, he didn't.

One day the farmer sent the boy to look after the sheep. He was to drive them to the top of a hill outside the village, where the grass grew long and sweet.

Hardly had the boy gone than he was back again, quite out of breath. He said, "Father! father! Get your gun! I saw a hare on the hill, as big as a horse!"

"A hare as big as a horse?" said his father. "I can't imagine that!"

"Well, perhaps it wasn't quite as big as a grown-up horse," said the boy. "But it was as big as a horse six weeks old."

"A hare as big as a horse six weeks old," said his father. "I can't imagine that!"

"Well, perhaps it wasn't quite as big as a horse six weeks old. But it was as big as a calf."

"A hare as big as a calf? I can't imagine that!"

"Well, perhaps it wasn't quite as big as a calf. But it was as big as a sheep."

"A hare as big as a sheep? I can't imagine that."

"Well, perhaps it wasn't quite as big as a sheep. But it was as big as a lamb."

"A hare as big as a lamb? I can't imagine that!"

"Well, perhaps it wasn't quite as big as a lamb. But it was as big as a cat."

"A hare as big as a cat? I can't imagine that."

"Well, perhaps it wasn't quite as big as a cat. But it was as big as a rat."

"A hare as big as a rat? I can't imagine that!"

"Well, perhaps it wasn't quite as big as a rat. But it was as big as a mouse."

"A hare as big as a mouse? I can't imagine that."

"Well, perhaps it wasn't quite as big as a mouse. But it was as big as a fly."

"A hare as big as a fly? Oh, my son! I don't think you saw anything at all!"

And he sent the little storyteller back to look after the sheep.

DON'T CUT THE LAWN!

Margaret Mahy

Mr Pomeroy went to his seaside cottage for the holidays. The sea was right, the sand was right, the sun was right, the salt was right. But outside his cottage the lawn had grown into a terrible, tussocky tangle. Mr Pomeroy decided that he would have to cut it.

He got out his lawnmower, Snapping Jack.

"Now for some fun!" said Snapping Jack. "Things have been very quiet lately. I've been wanting to get at that cheeky grass for weeks and weeks."

Mr Pomeroy began pushing the lawnmower, and the grass flew up and out. However, he had gone only a few steps when out of the tangly, tussocky jungle flew a lark crying:

"Don't cut the lawn, don't cut the lawn!
You will cut my little nestlings which have just been born."

Mr Pomeroy went to investigate and there, sure enough, were four baby larks in a nest on the ground.

"No need to worry, Madam!" cried Mr Pomeroy to the anxious mother. "We will go around your nest and cut the lawn further away."

So they went around the nest and started cutting the lawn further away.

"Now for it!" said Snapping Jack, snapping away happily.
But just then out jumped a mother hare crying:
"Don't cut the lawn, don't cut the lawn!
You will cut my little leveret which has just been born."
Mr Pomeroy went to investigate and there, sure enough,
was a little brown leveret, safe in his tussocky form.

"We'll have to go further away to do our mowing," Mr
Pomeroy said to Snapping Jack. So they went further away
and Mr Pomeroy said, "Now we'll really begin cutting this
lawn."

"Right!" said Snapping Jack. "And we'll have no mercy
on it."

But they had only just begun to have no mercy on the lawn when a tabby cat leaped out of the tussocky tangle and mewed at them:

"Don't cut the lawn, don't cut the lawn!
You will cut my little kittens which have just been born."

Mr Pomeroy went to investigate, and there, sure enough, were two stripy kittens in a little, golden, tussocky, tangly hollow.

"This place is more like a zoo than a lawn," grumbled Snapping Jack. "We'll go further away this time, but you must promise to be hard-hearted or the lawn will get the better of us."

"All right! If it happens again I'll be very hard-hearted," promised Mr Pomeroy.

They began to cut where the lawn was longest, lankiest, tangliest and most terribly tough and tussocky.

"I'm not going to take any notice of any interruptions this time," he said to himself firmly.

"We'll really get down to business," said Snapping Jack, beginning to champ with satisfaction.

Then something moved in the long, lank, tussocky tangle. Something slowly sat up and stared at them with jewelled eyes. It was a big mother dragon, as green as grass, as golden as a tussock. She looked at them and she hissed:

"Don't cut the lawn, don't cut the lawn!
You will cut my little dragon who has just been born."

There, among the leathery scraps of the shell of the dragon's egg, was a tiny dragon, as golden and glittering as a bejewelled evening bag. It blew out a tiny flame at them, just like a cigarette lighter.

"Isn't he clever for one so young!" exclaimed his loving mother. "Of course I can blow out a very big flame. I could

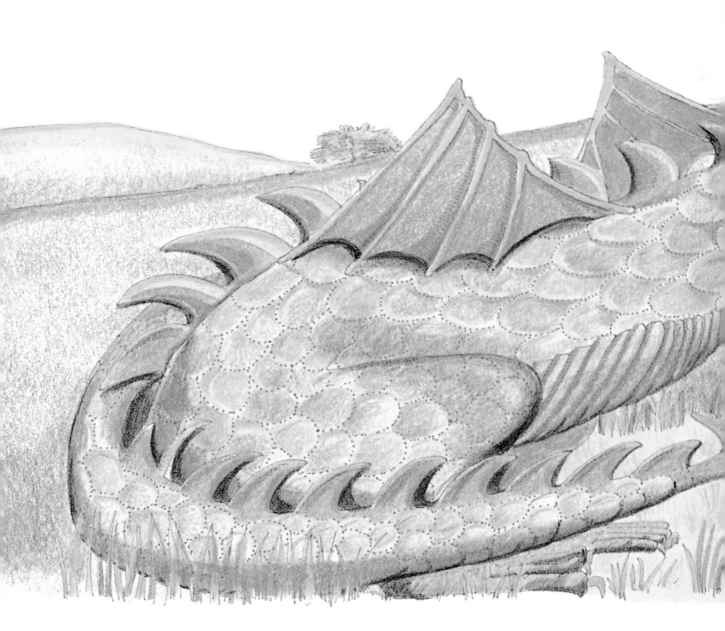

burn all this lawn in one blast if I wanted to. I could easily scorch off your eyebrows."

"Fire restrictions are on," croaked the alarmed Mr Pomeroy.

"Oh, I'm afraid that wouldn't stop me," said the dragon. "Not if I were upset about anything. And if you mowed my baby I'd be very upset. I'd probably breathe fire hot enough to melt a lawnmower!"

"What do *you* think?" Mr Pomeroy asked Snapping Jack.

"Let's leave it until next week," said Snapping Jack hurriedly. "We don't want to upset a loving mother, do we? Particularly one that breathes fire!"

So the lawn was left alone and Mr Pomeroy sat on his verandah enjoying the sun, or swam in the sea enjoying the salt water, and day by day he watched the cottage lawn grow more tussocky and more tangly. Then, one day, out of the tussocks and tangles flew four baby larks which began learning how to soar and sing as larks do. And out of the tussocks and tangles came a little hare which frolicked and frisked as hares do. And out of the tussocks and tangles came two stripy kittens which pounced and bounced as kittens do. And *then* out of the tussocks and tangles came a little dragon with golden scales and eyes like stars, and it laid its shining head on Mr Pomeroy's knee and told him some of the wonderful stories that only dragons know. Even Snapping Jack listened with interest.

"Fancy that!" he was heard to remark. "I'm glad I talked Mr Pomeroy out of mowing the lawn. Who'd ever believe a tussocky, tangly lawn could be home to so many creatures. There's more to a lawn than mere grass, you know!"

And Mr Pomeroy, the larks, the leveret, the kittens and the little dragon all agreed with him.

THE STEADFAST TIN SOLDIER

Hans Christian Andersen

There were once twenty-five tin soldiers, all of them brothers, for they had all been made from the same tin kitchen spoon. They shouldered arms, and looked straight before them, very smart in their red and blue uniforms. "Tin soldiers!" That was the very first thing that they heard in this world, when the lid of their box was taken off. A little boy had shouted this and clapped his hands; he had been given them as a birthday present, and now he set them out on the table. Each soldier was exactly like the next – except for one, which had only a single leg; he was the last to be moulded, and there was not quite enough tin left. Yet he stood just as well on his one leg as the others did on their two, and he is this story's hero.

On the table where they were placed there were many other toys, but the one which everyone noticed first was a paper castle. Through its little windows you could see right into the rooms. In front of it, tiny trees were arranged round a piece of mirror, which was meant to look like a lake. Swans made of wax seemed to float on its surface, and gaze at their white reflections. The whole scene was enchanting – and the prettiest thing of all was a girl who stood in the open doorway; she too was cut out of paper, but her gauzy skirt was of finest muslin; a narrow blue ribbon crossed her shoulder like a scarf, and was held by a shining sequin almost the size of her face. This charming little creature held both of her arms stretched out, for she was a dancer; indeed, one of her legs was raised so high in the air that the tin soldier could not see it at all; he thought that she had only one leg like himself.

"Now she would be just the right wife for me," he thought. "But she is so grand; she lives in a castle, and I have only a box – and there are five-and-twenty of us in that! There certainly isn't room for her. Still, I can try to make her acquaintance." So he lay down full-length behind a snuff-box which was on the table; from there he could easily watch the little paper dancer, who continued to stand on one leg without losing her balance.

When evening came, all the other tin soldiers were put in their box, and the children went to bed. Now the toys began to have games of their own; they played at visiting, and schools, and battles, and going to parties. The tin soldiers rattled in their box, for they wanted to join in, but they couldn't get the lid off. The nutcrackers turned somersaults, and the slate pencil squeaked on the slate; there was such a din that the canary woke up and took part in the talk – what's more, he did it in verse. The only two who didn't move were the tin soldier and the little dancer; she continued to stand on the point of her toe, with her arms held out; he stood just as steadily on his single leg – and never once did he take his eyes from her.

Now the clock struck twelve. Crack! – the lid flew off the snuff-box and up popped a little black goblin. There was no

snuff inside the box – it was a kind of trick, a jack-in-the-box.

"Tin soldier!" screeched the goblin. "Keep your eyes to yourself!"

But the tin soldier pretended not to hear.

"All right, just you wait till tomorrow!" said the goblin.

When morning came and the children were up again, the tin soldier was placed on the window ledge. The goblin may have been responsible, or perhaps a draught blowing through – anyhow, the window suddenly swung open, and out fell the tin soldier, all the three storeys to the ground. It was a dreadful fall! His leg pointed upwards, his head was down, and he came to a halt with his bayonet stuck between the paving stones.

The servant-girl and the little boy went to search in the street, but although they were almost treading on the soldier they somehow failed to see him. If he had called out, "Here I am!" they would have found him easily, but he didn't think it proper behaviour to cry out when he was in uniform.

Now it began to rain; the drops fell fast – it was a drenching shower. When it was over, a pair of urchins passed. "Look!" said one of them. "There's a tin soldier. Let's put him out to sea."

So they made a boat out of newspaper and put the tin soldier in the middle, and set it in the fast-flowing gutter at the edge of the street. Away he sped, and the two boys ran beside him clapping their hands. Goodness, what waves there were in that gutter-stream, what rolling tides! It had been a real downpour. The paper boat tossed up and down, sometimes whirling round and round, until the soldier felt quite giddy. But he remained as steadfast as ever, not moving a muscle, still looking straight in front of him, still shouldering arms.

All at once the boat entered a tunnel under the pavement. Oh, it was dark, quite as dark as it was in the box at home. "Wherever am I going now?" the tin soldier wondered. "Yes, it must be the goblin's doing. Ah! If only that young lady were here with me in the boat, I wouldn't care if it were twice as dark."

Suddenly, from its home in the tunnel, out rushed a large water-rat. "Have you a passport?" it demanded. "No entry without a passport!"

But the tin soldier said never a word; he only gripped his musket more tightly than ever. The boat rushed onwards, and behind it rushed the rat in fast pursuit. Ugh! How it ground its teeth, and yelled to the sticks and straws, "Stop him! Stop him! He hasn't paid his toll! He hasn't shown his passport!"

There was no stopping the boat, though, for the stream ran stronger and stronger. The tin soldier could just see a bright glimpse of daylight far ahead where the end of the tunnel must be, but at the same time he heard a roaring noise which well might have frightened a bolder man. Just imagine! At the end of the tunnel the stream thundered down into a great canal. It was as dreadful for him as a plunge down a giant waterfall would be for us.

But how could he stop? Already he was close to the terrible edge. The boat raced on, and the poor tin soldier held himself as stiffly as he could – no one could say of him that he even blinked an eye.

Suddenly the little vessel whirled round three or four times, and filled with water right to the brim; what could it do but sink! The tin soldier stood in water up to his neck; deeper and deeper sank the boat, softer and softer grew the paper, until at last the water closed over the soldier's head. He thought of the lovely little dancer whom he would never see again, and in his ears rang the words of a song:

"Onward, onward, warrior brave!
Fear not danger, nor the grave."

Then the paper boat collapsed entirely. Out fell the tin soldier – and he was promptly swallowed up by a fish.

Oh, how dark it was in the fish's stomach! It was even worse than the tunnel, and very much more cramped. But the tin soldier's courage remained unchanged; there he lay, as steadfast as ever, his musket still at his shoulder. The fish swam wildly about, twisted and turned, and then became quite still. Something flashed through like a streak of

44

lightning – then all around was cheerful daylight, and a voice cried out, "The tin soldier!"

The fish had been caught, taken to market, sold and carried into the kitchen, where the cook had cut it open with a large knife. Now she picked up the soldier, holding him round his waist between her finger and thumb, and took him into the living room, so that all the family could see the remarkable character who had travelled about inside a fish. But the tin soldier was not at all proud. They stood him up on the table, and there – well, the world is full of wonders! – he saw that he was in the very same room where his adventures had started; there were the very same children; there were the very same toys; there was the fine paper castle with the graceful little dancer at the door. She was still poised on one leg, with the other raised high in the air. Ah, she was steadfast too. The tin soldier was deeply moved; he would have liked to weep tin tears, only that

would not have been soldierly behaviour. He looked at her, and she looked at him, but not a word passed between them.

And then a strange thing happened. One of the small boys picked up the tin soldier and threw him into the stove. He had no reason for doing this; it must have been the snuff-box goblin's fault.

The tin soldier stood framed in a blaze of light. The heat was intense, but whether this came from the fire or his burning love, he could not tell. His bright colours were now gone – but whether they had been washed away by his journey, or through his sorrow, none could say. He looked at the pretty little dancer, and she looked at him; he felt that he was melting away, but he still stood steadfast, shouldering arms. Suddenly the door flew open; a gust of air caught the little paper girl, and she flew like a sylph right into the stove, straight to the waiting tin soldier; there she flashed into flame and vanished.

The soldier presently melted down to a lump of tin, and the next day, when the maid raked out the ashes she found him – in the shape of a little tin heart. And the dancer? All that they found was her sequin, and that was as black as soot.

JACK AND THE BEANSTALK

Joseph Jacobs

There was once upon a time a poor widow who had an only son named Jack, and a cow named Milky-white. And all they had to live on was the milk the cow gave every morning, which they carried to the market and sold. But one morning Milky-white gave no milk, and they didn't know what to do.

"What shall we do, what shall we do?" said the widow, wringing her hands.

"Cheer up, mother, I'll go and get work somewhere," said Jack.

"We've tried that before, and nobody would take you," said his mother; "we must sell Milky-white and with the money start a shop, or something."

"All right, mother," says Jack; "it's market-day today, and I'll soon sell Milky-white, and then we'll see what we can do."

So he took the cow's halter in his hand, and off he

started. He hadn't gone far when he met a funny-looking old man, who said to him: "Good morning, Jack."

"Good morning to you," said Jack, and wondered how he knew his name.

"Well, Jack, and where are you off to?" said the man.

"I'm going to market to sell our cow here."

"You look the proper sort of chap to sell cows," said the man; "and do you know how many beans make five?"

"Two in each hand and one in your mouth," says Jack, as sharp as a needle.

"Right you are," says the man, "and here they are, the very beans themselves," he went on, pulling out of his pocket a number of strange-looking beans. "As you are so sharp," says he, "I don't mind doing a swop with you – your cow for these beans."

"Go along," says Jack; "wouldn't you like it?"

"Ah! you don't know what these beans are," said the man; "if you plant them overnight, by morning they grow right up to the sky."

"Really?" said Jack; "you don't say so."

"Yes, that is so, and if it doesn't turn out to be true you can have your cow back."

"Right," says Jack, and hands him over Milky-white's halter and pockets the beans.

Back goes Jack home, and as he hadn't gone very far it wasn't dusk by the time he got to his door.

"Back already, Jack?" said his mother; "I see you haven't got Milky-white, so you've sold her. How much did you get for her?"

"You'll never guess, mother," says Jack.

"No, you don't say. Good boy! Five pounds, ten, fifteen, no, it can't be twenty."

"I told you you couldn't guess. What do you say to these beans; they're magical, plant them overnight and –"

"What!" says Jack's mother, "have you been such a fool, such a dolt, such an idiot, as to give away my Milky-white, the best milker in the parish, and prime beef to boot, for a set of paltry beans? Take that! Take that! Take that! And as for your precious beans, here they go out of the window. And now off with you to bed. Not a sup shall you drink, and not a bit shall you swallow this very night."

So Jack went upstairs to his little room in the attic, and sad and sorry he was, to be sure, as much for his mother's sake, as for the loss of his supper.

At last he dropped off to sleep.

When he woke up, the room looked so funny. The sun was shining into part of it, and yet all the rest was quite dark and shady. So Jack jumped up and dressed himself and went to the window. And what do you think he saw? Why, the beans his mother had thrown out of the window into the garden had sprung up into a big beanstalk which went up and up and up till it reached the sky. So the man spoke truth after all.

The beanstalk grew up quite close past Jack's window, so all he had to do was to open it and give a jump on to the beanstalk which ran up just like a big ladder. So Jack climbed, and he climbed and he climbed and he climbed and he climbed and he climbed and he climbed till at last he reached the sky. And when he got there he found a long broad road going as straight as a dart. So he walked along and he walked along and he walked along till he came to a great big tall house, and on the doorstep there was a great big tall woman.

"Good morning, mum," says Jack, quite polite-like. "Could you be so kind as to give me some breakfast?" For he hadn't had anything to eat, you know, the night before and was as hungry as a hunter.

"It's breakfast you want, is it?" says the great big tall woman, "it's breakfast you'll be if you don't move off from here. My man is an ogre and there's nothing he likes better than boys broiled on toast. You'd better be moving on or he'll soon be coming."

"Oh! please, mum, do give me something to eat, mum. I've had nothing to eat since yesterday morning, really and truly, mum," says Jack. "I may as well be broiled as die of hunger."

Well, the ogre's wife was not half so bad after all. So she took Jack into the kitchen, and gave him a hunk of bread and cheese and a jug of milk. But Jack hadn't half finished these when thump! thump! thump! the whole house began to tremble with the noise of someone coming.

"Goodness gracious me! It's my old man," said the ogre's wife, "what on earth shall I do? Come along quick and jump in here." And she bundled Jack into the oven just as the ogre came in.

He was a big one, to be sure. At his belt he had three calves strung up by the heels, and he unhooked them and threw them down on the table and said: "Here, wife, broil me a couple of these for breakfast. Ah! what's this I smell?

"Fee-fi-fo-fum,
I smell the blood of an Englishman,
Be he alive, or be he dead
I'll have his bones to grind my bread."

"Nonsense, dear," said his wife, "you're dreaming. Or perhaps you smell the scraps of that little boy you liked so much for yesterday's dinner. Here, you go and have a wash and tidy up, and by the time you come back your breakfast'll be ready for you."

So off the ogre went, and Jack was just going to jump out of the oven and run away when the woman told him not. "Wait till he's asleep," says she; "he always has a doze after breakfast."

Well, the ogre had his breakfast, and after that he goes to a big chest and takes out of it a couple of bags of gold, and down he sits and counts till at last his head began to nod and he began to snore till the whole house shook again.

Then Jack crept out on tiptoe from his oven, and as he

was passing the ogre he took one of the bags of gold under his arm, and off he pelters till he came to the beanstalk, and then he threw down the bag of gold, which, of course, fell into his mother's garden, and then he climbed down till at last he got home and told his mother and showed her the gold and said: "Well, mother, wasn't I right about the beans? They are really magical, you see."

So they lived on the bag of gold for some time, but at last they came to the end of it, and Jack made up his mind to try his luck once more at the top of the beanstalk. So one fine morning he rose up early, and got on to the beanstalk, and he climbed and he climbed and he climbed and he climbed and he climbed and he climbed till at last he came out on to the road again and up to the great big tall house he had been to before. There, sure enough, was the great big tall woman a-standing on the doorstep.

"Good morning, mum," says Jack, as bold as brass, "could you be so good as to give me something to eat?"

"Go away, my boy," said the big tall woman, "or else my man will eat you up for breakfast. But aren't you the youngster who came here once before? Do you know, that very day my man missed one of his bags of gold."

"That's strange, mum," said Jack, "I dare say I could tell you something about that, but I'm so hungry I can't speak till I've had something to eat."

Well, the big tall woman was so curious that she took him in and gave him something to eat. But he had scarcely begun munching it as slowly as he could when thump! thump! they heard the giant's footstep, and his wife hid Jack away in the oven.

All happened as it did before. In came the ogre as he did before, said: "Fee-fi-fo-fum", and had his breakfast of three broiled oxen. Then he said: "Wife, bring me the hen that lays the golden eggs." So she brought it, and the ogre said: "Lay," and it laid an egg all of gold. And then the ogre began to nod his head, and to snore till the house shook.

Then Jack crept out of the oven on tiptoe and caught hold of the golden hen, and was off before you could say "Jack Robinson". But this time the hen gave a cackle which woke the ogre, and just as Jack got out of the house he heard him calling: "Wife, wife, what have you done with

my golden hen?"

And the wife said: "Why, my dear?"

But that was all Jack heard, for he rushed off to the beanstalk and climbed down like a house on fire. And when he got home he showed his mother the hen and said "Lay" to it; and it laid a golden egg every time he said "Lay."

Well, Jack was not content, and it wasn't very long before he determined to have another try at his luck up there at the top of the beanstalk. So one fine morning, he rose up early, and got on to the beanstalk, and he climbed and he climbed and he climbed and he climbed till he got to the top. But this time he knew better than to go straight to the ogre's house. And when he got near it, he waited behind a bush till he saw the ogre's wife come out with a pail to get some water, and then he crept into the house and got into the copper. He hadn't been there long when he heard thump! thump! thump! as before, and in came the ogre and his wife.

"Fee-fi-fo-fum, I smell the blood of an Englishman," cried out the ogre. "I smell him, wife, I smell him."

"Do you, my dearie?" says the ogre's wife. "Then, if it's that little rogue that stole your gold and the hen that laid the golden eggs he's sure to have got into the oven." And they both rushed to the oven. But Jack wasn't there, luckily, and the ogre's wife said: "There you are again with your fee-fi-fo-fum. Why, of course, it's the boy you caught last night that I've just broiled for your breakfast. How forgetful I am, and how careless you are not to know the difference between live and dead after all these years."

So the ogre sat down to the breakfast and ate it, but every now and then he would mutter: "Well, I could have sworn —" and he'd get up and search the larder and the cupboards and everything, only, luckily, he didn't think of the copper.

After breakfast was over, the ogre called out: "Wife, wife, bring me my golden harp." So she brought it and put it on the table before him. Then he said: "Sing!" and the golden harp sang most beautifully. And it went on singing till the ogre fell asleep, and began to snore like thunder.

Then Jack lifted up the copper-lid very quietly and got down like a mouse and crept on hands and knees till he came to the table, when up he crawled, caught hold of the golden harp and dashed with it towards the door. But the harp called out quite loud: "Master! Master!" and the ogre woke up just in time to see Jack running off with his harp.

Jack ran as fast as he could, and the ogre came rushing after, and would soon have caught him only Jack had a start and dodged him a bit and knew where he was going. When he got to the beanstalk the ogre was no more than twenty yards away when suddenly he saw Jack disappear like, and when he came to the end of the road he saw Jack underneath climbing down for dear life. Well, the ogre didn't like trusting himself to such a ladder, and he stood and waited, so Jack got another start. But just then the harp cried out: "Master! Master!" and the ogre swung himself down on to the beanstalk, which shook with his weight. Down climbs Jack, and after him climbed the ogre. By this time Jack had climbed down and climbed down and climbed down till he was very nearly home. So he called out: "Mother! Mother! bring me an axe, bring me an axe." And his mother came rushing out with the axe in her hand, but when she came to the beanstalk she stood stock still with fright, for there she saw the ogre with his legs just through the clouds.

But Jack jumped down and got hold of the axe and gave a chop at the beanstalk which cut it half in two. The ogre felt the beanstalk shake and quiver, so he stopped to see what was the matter. Then Jack gave another chop with the axe, and the beanstalk was cut in two and began to topple over. Then the ogre fell down and broke his crown, and the beanstalk came toppling after.

Then Jack showed his mother his golden harp, and what with showing that and selling the golden eggs, Jack and his mother became very rich, and he married a great princess, and they lived happy ever after.

THE
SEA BABY

Eleanor Farjeon

The stocking-basket was empty. For once there was
nothing to darn. The Old Nurse had told so many
stories, that she had mended all the holes made by Doris
and Mary Matilda, and even by Ronnie and Roley.
Tomorrow they would make some more, of course, but
tonight the Old Nurse sat with her hands folded in her lap,
and watched the children fall asleep by fire-light.

Only one of them kept awake. Mary Matilda would not
go to sleep. She was not cross, she was not ill, there was no
reason at all except that she was wide awake. She kept on
standing up in her cot and laughing at the Old Nurse over
the bars. And when the Old Nurse came and laid her down
and tucked her up, she turned over and laughed at the Old
Nurse *between* the cot-bars.

"Go to sleep, Mary Matilda," said the Old Nurse in her
hush-hush voice. "Shut your eyes, my darling, and go to
sleep."

But Mary Matilda couldn't, or if she could, she wouldn't.
And at last the Old Nurse did what she very seldom did: she
came over to Mary Matilda, and took her out of the cot,

and carried her to the fire, and rocked her on her knee.

"Can't you go to sleep, baby?" she crooned. "Can't you go to sleep, then? Ah, you're just my Sea-Baby over again! *She* never went to sleep, either, all the time I nursed her. And she was the very first I ever nursed. I've never told anybody about her since, but I'll tell you, Mary Matilda. So shut your eyes and listen, while I tell about my Sea-Baby."

I couldn't tell you when it happened: it was certainly a long time after the Flood, and I know I was only about ten years old, and had never left the Norfolk village on the sea-coast where I was born. My father was a fisherman, and a tiller of the land; and my mother kept the house and span the wool and linen for our clothes. But that tells us nothing, for fathers have provided the food, and mothers have kept the house, since the beginning of things. So don't go asking any more when it was that I nursed my very first baby.

It happened like this, Mary Matilda. Our cottage stood near the edge of the cliff, and at high tide the sea came right up to the foot, but at low tide it ran so far back that it

seemed almost too far to follow it. People said that once, long ago, the sea had not come in so close; and that the cliff had gone out many miles farther. And on the far end of the cliff had stood another village. But after the Flood all that part of the cliff was drowned under the sea, and the village along with it. And there, said the people, the village still lay, far out to sea under the waves; and on stormy nights, they said, you could hear the church bells ringing in the church tower below the water. Ah, don't you start laughing at your old Nanny now! We knew it was true, I tell you. And one day something happened to prove it.

A big storm blew up over our part of the land; the biggest storm that any of us could remember, so big that we thought the Flood had come again. The sky was as black as night all day long, and the wind blew so hard that it drove a strong man backwards, and the rain poured down so that you only had to hold a pitcher out of the window for a second, and when you took it in it was flowing over, and the thunder growled and crackled so that we had to make signs to each other, for talking was no use, and the lightning flashed so bright that my mother could thread her needle by it. That *was* a storm, that was! My mother was frightened, but my father, who was weather-wise, watched the sky and said from time to time, "I think that'll come out all right." And so it did. The lightning and thunder flashed and rolled themselves away into the distance, the rain stopped, the wind died down, the sky cleared up for a beautiful evening, and the sun turned all the vast wet sands to a sheet of gold as far as the eye could see. Yes, and farther! For a wonder had happened during the storm. The sea had been driven back so far that it had vanished out of sight, and sands were laid bare that no living man or woman had viewed before. And there, far, far across the golden beach, lay a tiny village, shining in the setting sun.

Think of our excitement, Mary Matilda! It was the drowned village of long ago, come back to the light of day.

Everybody gathered on the shore to look at it. And suddenly I began to run towards it, and all the other children followed me. At first our parents called, "Come back! Come back! The sea may come rolling in before you can get there." But we were too eager to see the village for

ourselves, and in the end the big folk felt the same about it; and they came running after the children across the sands. As we drew nearer, the little houses became plainer, looking like blocks of gold in the evening light; and the little streets appeared like golden brooks, and the church spire in the middle was like a point of fire.

For all my little legs, I was the first to reach the village. I had had a start of the others, and could always run fast as a child and never tire. We had long stopped running, of course, for the village was so far out that our breath would not last. But I was still walking rapidly when I reached the village and turned a corner. As I did so, I heard one of the big folk cry, "Oh, look! Yonder lies the sea." I glanced ahead, and did see, on the far horizon beyond the village, the shining line of the sea that had gone so far away. Then I heard another grown-up cry, "Take care! Take care! Who knows when it may begin to roll back again? We have come far, and oh, suppose the sea should overtake us before we can reach home!" Then, peeping round my corner, I saw everybody take fright and turn tail, running as hard as they could across the mile or so of sands they had just crossed. But nobody had noticed me, or thought of me; no doubt my own parents thought I was one of the band of running children, and so they left me alone there, with all the little village to myself.

What a lovely time I had, going into the houses, up and down the streets, and through the church. Everything was left as it had been, and seemed ready for someone to come to; the flowers were blooming in the gardens, the fruit was hanging on the trees, the tables were spread for the next meal, a pot was standing by the kettle on the hearth in one house, and in another there were toys upon the floor. And when I began to go upstairs to the other rooms, I found in every bed someone asleep. Grandmothers and grandfathers, mothers and fathers, young men and young women, boys and girls: all so fast asleep, that there was no waking them. And at last, in a little room at the top of a house, I found a baby in a cradle, wide awake.

She was the sweetest baby I had ever seen. Her eyes were as blue as the sea that had covered them so long, her skin as white as the foam, and her little round head as gold as the sands in the evening sunlight. When she saw me, she sat up in her cradle, and crowed with delight. I knelt down beside her, held out my arms, and she cuddled into them with a little gleeful chuckle. I carried her about the room, dancing her up and down in my arms, calling her my baby, my pretty Sea-Baby, and showing her the things in the room and out of the window. But as we were looking out of the window at a bird's nest in a tree, I seemed to see the shining line of water on the horizon begin to move.

"The sea is coming in!" I thought. "I must hurry back before it catches us." And I flew out of the house with the Sea-Baby in my arms, and ran as hard as I could out of the

village, and followed the crowd of golden footsteps on the sands, anxious to get home soon. When I had to pause to get my breath, I ventured to glance over my shoulder, and there behind me lay the little village, still glinting in the sun. On I ran again, and after a while was forced to stop a second time. Once more I glanced behind me, and this time the village was not to be seen: it had disappeared beneath the tide of the sea, which was rolling in behind me.

Then how I scampered over the rest of the way! I reached home just as the tiny wavelets, which run in front of the big waves, began to lap my ankles, and I scrambled up the cliff, with the Sea-Baby in my arms, and got indoors, panting for breath. Nobody was at home, for as it happened they were all out looking for me. So I took my baby upstairs, and put her to bed in my own bed, and got her some warm milk. But she turned from the milk, and wouldn't drink it. She only seemed to want to laugh and play with me. So I did for a little while, and then I told her she must go to sleep. But she only laughed some more, and went on playing.

"Shut your eyes, baby," I said to her, "hush-hush! Hush-hush!" (just as my own mother said to me). But the baby didn't seem to understand, and went on laughing.

Then I said, "You're a very naughty baby" (as my mother sometimes used to say to me). But she didn't mind that either, and just went on laughing. So in the end I had to laugh too, and play with her.

My mother heard us, when she came into the house; and she ran up to find me, delighted that I was safe. What was her surprise to find the baby with me! She asked me where it had come from, and I told her; and she called my father, and he stood scratching his head, as most men do when they aren't quite sure about a thing.

"I want to keep it for my own, Mother," I said.

"Well, we can't turn it out now it's in," said my mother. "But you'll have to look after it yourself, mind."

I wanted nothing better! I'd always wanted to nurse things, whether it was a log of wood, or a kitten, or my mother's shawl rolled into a dumpy bundle. And now I had a little live baby of my own to nurse. How I did enjoy myself that week! I did everything for it; dressed and undressed it, washed it and combed its hair; and played and danced with it, and talked with it and walked with it. And I tried to give it its meals, but it wouldn't eat; and I tried to put it to sleep, but it wouldn't shut its eyes. No, not for anything I could do, though I sang to it, and rocked it, and told it little stories.

It didn't worry me much, for I knew no better: but it worried my mother, and I heard her say to my father, "There's something queer about that child. I don't know, I'm sure!"

On the seventh night after the storm, I woke up suddenly from my dreams, as I lay in bed with my baby beside me. It was very late, my parents had long gone to bed themselves, and what had wakened me I did not know, for I heard no sound at all. The moon was very bright, and filled the square of my window-pane with silver light; and through the air outside I saw something swimming – I thought at first it was a white cloud, but as it reached my open window I saw it was a lady, moving along the air as though she were swimming in water. And the strange thing was that her eyes were fast shut; so that as her white arms moved out and in she seemed to be swimming not only in the air, but in her sleep.

She swam straight through my open window to the bedside, and there she came to rest, letting her feet down upon the floor like a swimmer setting his feet on the sands under his body. The lady leaned over the bed with her shut eyes, and took my wide-awake baby in her arms.

"*Hush-hush! Hush-hush!*" she said; and the sound of her voice was not like my mother's voice when she said it, but like the waves washing the shore on a still night; such a peaceful sound, the sort of sound that might have been the first sound made in the world, or else the last. You couldn't help wanting to sleep as you heard her say it. I felt my head begin to nod, and as it grew heavier and heavier, I noticed that my Sea-Baby's eyelids were beginning to droop too. Before I could see any more, I fell asleep; and when I awoke in the morning my baby had gone. "Where to, Mary Matilda? Ah, you mustn't ask me that! I only know she must have gone where all babies go when they go to sleep. Go to sleep. Hush-hush! *Hush-hush! Go to sleep!*"

Mary Matilda had gone to sleep at last. The Old Nurse laid her softly in her cot, turned down the light, and crept out of the nursery.

PRICKETY PRACKETY

Diana Ross

There was once a hen called Prickety Prackety. She was a little golden brown bantam hen, and she walked about the garden on the tips of her toes – and she pecked here and pecked there and was busy and gay the whole day long.

And once a day she felt like laying an egg.

Away she went to the hen-house: "Cluck, Cluck, Cluck!" And she'd climb into the nesting box and fluff herself out and make gentle noises in her throat as soft as her own pretty feathers, and she'd sit, and she'd blink her eyes and go into a dozy-cosy and then: "Cluck, Cluck, Cluck-a-Cluck-a-Cluck!"

What a surprise! What joy! An egg! A pretty brown speckledy egg! Away she would go, not a thought in her head, peck here, peck there, on the tips of her toes.

And Anne would come at tea-time to collect the eggs, and when she saw the brown egg she would say:

"Oh! You good Mrs Prickety Prackety, you good little hen." Because Prickety Prackety was the only hen to lay brown eggs, so Anne knew that it was hers. And she would throw her out an extra handful of corn. One good turn deserves another.

But one day Prickety Prackety felt different. She felt like laying an egg. Oh, yes! But somehow not in the hen-house. So away she went by herself.

"Where are you going to, Prickety Prackety?" called Chanticleer the golden cock.

"I am going to mind my own business," she said and tossed her head. Chanticleer ran and gave her a little peck, not a hard peck, but enough of a peck to show that although he loved her dearly he wouldn't let her answer him so rudely.

But Prickety Prackety paid no attention to him. She fluttered her feathers and cried "Cloak!" because she knew he would expect it, and then she ran away, her head in the air.

"Prickety Prackety, where are you going?"

It was good sister Partlet, the old black hen, wanting her to share a dustbath near the cinder-pit.

"I am going to mind my own business," said Prickety Prackety nodding pleasantly to Partlet, and Partlet ruffled the dust in her feathers and smiled to herself.

Prickety Prackety left the garden and came to the orchard. The grass was very green underneath the apple trees and the blossom was just coming out.

"Prickety Prackety, where are you going?" cried the white ducks rootling in the grass.

"I am going to mind my own business," she said.

Beside the privet hedge was an old rusty drum.

It had been used last year to cover up the rhubarb, but now it was lying on its side and a jungle of nettles had grown up all round it.

And Prickety Prackety crept through the jungle of nettles, into the oil drum and clucked contentedly to find a few wisps of straw and dried grass. The geese and ducks smiled at each other and went on nibbling the grass in the orchard.

"Prickety Prackety has stolen a nest. I wonder if they will find it?" they thought to themselves.

Every day for twelve days Prickety Prackety disappeared into the oil drum.

Every day Chanticleer said, "Prickety Prackety, where are you going?"

Every day Partlet said, "Prickety Prackety, where are you going?"

Every day the geese and ducks said, "Prickety Prackety, where are you going?"

And every day Prickety Prackety gave the same answer with a toss of her head: "I am going to mind my own business."

And every day at tea-time Anne would come in shaking her head.

"No eggs from Prickety Prackety. She's gone right off. And just when she was doing so well too."

But worse was to come.

On the thirteenth day Prickety Prackety took a long drink and ate as much as she could when Anne put out the hot mash. And then she walked away looking *very* important.

"Where are you going, Prickety Prackety?" said Chanticleer.

"Where are you going, Prickety Prackety?" said Partlet.

"Where are you going, Prickety Prackety?" said the white ducks.

"Where are you going to, Prickety Prackety?" said the geese, following after her as if she were a procession.

But Prickety Prackety didn't even answer. She pranced along, her eyes shining.

That evening Anne came into the kitchen and said:

"Now I know why Prickety Prackety seemed to go off laying. She has stolen a nest. I shall have to go and find it."

So next day after she had put out the chicken food Anne began to look for Prickety Prackety.

She looked in the shrubbery. She looked in the vegetable garden. She looked in the sheds and outhouses. She looked along the hedges, looked in the orchard, but she didn't see Prickety Prackety, although Prickety Prackety saw her.

And every morning when it was first light and the other hens were still asleep shut up in the hen-house, Prickety Prackety would creep out of her jungle of nettles.

"Where are you going to, Prickety Prackety?" asked the little wild birds, the sparrows and finches, the blackbirds and the thrushes. But Prickety Prackety seemed not to hear, but would peck here and there, gorging herself on grubs and grass and any remains of chicken food overlooked by the others. She would drink and drink from the bowl of water by the back door, and as she lifted her head the rising sun would shine into her eyes, and then back she would go through her jungle of nettles into the oil drum, and not the least glimpse of her to be seen when the rest of the world were about.

A week went by, and another, and the blossom on the apple trees was falling so that when the soft wind blew it looked like drifting snow. And still Prickety Prackety hid in her nest.

"Have you seen Prickety Prackety?" said Chanticleer to Partlet.

"Oh! She's around somewhere," said Partlet, flaunting her feathers.

"Have you seen Prickety Prackety?" said Partlet to the ducks.

"Oh! I expect she's around somewhere," they said.

"Have you seen Prickety Prackety?" asked the ducks of the geese.

"We mind our own businesssssss," hissed the geese.

And Anne, in the kitchen yard, said: "Now, let me see. It's gone all of two weeks since Prickety Prackety stole her nest. She ought to be out come Friday. I wonder how many will hatch?"

On Friday when the sun rose the sky was quiet and clear.

Prickety Prackety crept out into the orchard shaking the dew from the nettles as she passed, so she looked like a golden hen set with diamonds.

She pecked and pranced and pecked and drank, and cocked her eye at the sun, and then she went back to her eggs, her twelve brown eggs lying on the straw in the cool green shadow of the oil drum and nettles.

She stood, her head on one side, and listened.

Tap-tap, and the smooth round surface of the nearest egg was broken and a tiny jag of shell moved and was still.

"Cluck, Cluck, Cluck, Cluck!" crooned Prickety Prackety, deep in her throat and, very satisfied, she settled on her eggs.

That evening Anne went out at tea-time.

"Coop, Coop, Coop!" she cried, the corn measure in her hand, and from every side the hens came running.

"Coop, Coop, Coop!" cried Anne.

Then who should creep out of the nettles but Prickety Prackety. "Cluck, Cluck, Cluck," she said. And out of the nettles crept, one, two, three, four, five, six, seven, eight, nine, ten, eleven, twelve little tiny, tiny chicks, so small, so tiny, so quick, so golden, so yellow – Oh, what a pretty sight!

"Well, you got them at last, Prickety Prackety," said the geese.

"And very nice too," said the ducks.

And Prickety Prackety led her family out of the orchard towards the yard. "Coop, Coop, Coop, Coop," cried Anne, scattering the corn.

But then she saw Prickety Prackety tripping towards her with one, two, three, four, five, six, seven, eight, nine, ten, eleven, twelve – yes, with twelve – tiny chicks, like little yellow clouds all about her:

"Oh!" she cried, and ran to the house.

"Caroline, Johnny, William, come quick. Prickety Prackety has hatched her chicks."

And everyone came running.

"Oh! Prickety Prackety, you *good* little hen!" And how they scattered the corn for her. But Anne was busy getting ready the special coop they kept for hens who had chicks; and they called it the Nursery Coop, for here the chicks would be safe from the cats and dogs and crows.

Very gently they lifted Prickety Prackety, and all the chicks came running as she cried to them; "Cluck, Cluck, Cluck!"

"I reckon you don't run that fast when your Mum calls you," said Anne – and the children laughed. And they all helped to carry the coop into the orchard, where the trees would shade it. And when at last Anne and the children were gone Partlet came busily by.

"A lot of trouble, but worth it. They're a fine lot, Prickety Prackety." And she nodded her head with approval.

And as for Chanticleer, he came stalking up glowing in the evening sun, and stood high on his toes, head cocked, looking at Prickety Prackety and the tiny heads poking in and out of her feathers. And then:

"Cock-a-Dooooooodle Doooooooooo. Just look at my good wife, Prickety Prackety, and all our sons and daughters. Cock-a-Dooooooodle Doooooooo."

It was like a fanfare of trumpets.

And Prickety Prackety blinked her eyes and smiled.

THE GIANT WHO THREW TANTRUMS

David L. Harrison

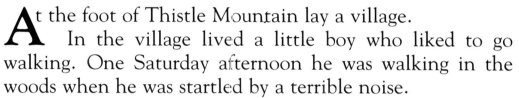

At the foot of Thistle Mountain lay a village.
In the village lived a little boy who liked to go
walking. One Saturday afternoon he was walking in the
woods when he was startled by a terrible noise.

He scrambled quickly behind a bush.

Before long a huge giant came stamping down the path.

He looked upset.

"Tanglebangled ringlepox!" the giant bellowed. He
banged his head against a tree until the leaves shook off like
snowflakes. "Franglewhangled whippersnack!" the giant
roared. Yanking up the tree, he whirled it around his head
and knocked down twenty-seven other trees.

Muttering to himself, he stalked up the path towards the
top of Thistle Mountain.

The little boy hurried home.

"I just saw a giant throwing a tantrum!" he told everyone
in the village.

They only smiled.

"There's no such thing as a giant," the mayor assured
him.

"He knocked down twenty-seven trees," said the little
boy.

"Must have been a tornado," the weatherman said with a nod. "Happens around here all the time."

The next Saturday afternoon the little boy again went walking. Before long he heard a horrible noise. Quick as lightning, he slipped behind a tree.

Soon the same giant came storming down the path. He still looked upset.

"Pollywogging frizzelsnatch!" he yelled. Throwing himself down, he pounded the ground with both fists.

Boulders bounced like hailstones.

Scowling, the giant puckered his lips into an 'O'.

He drew in his breath sharply. It sounded like somebody slurping soup.

"Pooh!" he cried.

Grabbing his left foot with both hands, the giant hopped on his right foot up the path towards the top of Thistle Mountain.

The little boy hurried home.

"That giant's at it again," he told everyone. "He threw such a tantrum that the ground trembled!"

"Must have been an earthquake," the police chief said. "Happens around here sometimes."

The next Saturday afternoon the little boy again went walking. Before long he heard a frightening noise.

He dropped down behind a rock.

Soon the giant came fuming down the path. When he

reached the little boy's rock, he puckered his lips into an 'O'. He drew in his breath sharply with a loud, rushing-wind sound. "Phooey!" he cried. "I *never* get it right!"

The giant held his breath until his face turned blue and his eyes rolled up. "Fozzlehumper backawacket!" he panted. Then he lumbered up the path towards the top of Thistle Mountain.

The little boy followed him. Up and up and up he

climbed to the very top of Thistle Mountain.

There he discovered a huge cave. A surprising sound was coming from it. The giant was crying!

"All I want is to whistle," he sighed through his tears. "But every time I try, it comes out wrong!"

The little boy had just learned to whistle. He knew how hard it could be. He stepped inside the cave.

The giant looked surprised. "How did *you* get here?"

"I know what you're doing wrong," the little boy said.

When the giant heard that, he leaned down and put his hands on his knees.

"Tell me at once!" he begged.

"You have to stop throwing tantrums," the little boy told him.

"I promise!" said the giant, who didn't want anyone to think he had poor manners.

"Pucker your lips . . ." the little boy said.

"I always do!" the giant assured him.

"Then blow," the little boy added.

"Blow?"

"Blow."

The giant looked as if he didn't believe it. He puckered his lips into an 'O'. He blew. Out came a long, low whistle. It sounded like a railway engine. The giant smiled.

He shouted, "I whistled! Did you hear that? I whistled!"

Taking the little boy's hand, he danced in a circle.

"You're a good friend," the giant said.

"Thank you," said the little boy. "Perhaps some time we can whistle together. But just now I have to go. It's my suppertime."

The giant stood before his cave and waved goodbye.

The little boy seldom saw the giant after that. But the

giant kept his promise about not throwing tantrums.

"We never have earthquakes," the mayor liked to say.

"Haven't had a tornado in ages," the weatherman would add.

Now and then they heard a long, low whistle somewhere in the distance.

"Must be a train," the police chief would say.

But the little boy knew his friend the giant was walking up the path towards the top of Thistle Mountain — whistling.

PUSS IN BOOTS

Charles Perrault

Many, many years ago there lived a miller who had a mill, a donkey, a cat, and three sons. So when he died it was very simple to divide up his belongings. The mill went to the eldest son, the donkey went to the second son, and to the youngest son went the cat.

As you might imagine, the youngest son was not happy about this. He grumbled about it to himself. "What am I going to do?" he wondered. "I've nothing but a cat for my fortune. It's all very well for my brothers. With the mill and the donkey they'll earn their living well enough. But what about me?"

Now, the cat overheard what his master was saying, and to the young man's astonishment he spoke. "Don't worry, master," he said. "You won't starve. I have a plan."

"*You* have a plan?" cried the young man. "But what can *you* do?"

"Never mind about that, master," said the cat. "All I shall need is a sack . . . and a pair of boots. Ask no more questions. Do as I ask, and you'll find you're not half as badly off as you thought."

The youngest son remembered that the cat had always been extraordinarily clever; that is, when it came to catching rats or mice. He'd seen the cat lying in the flourbin, pretending to be dead . . . until a rat came unwisely to nibble at the flour. It was impossible to imagine a cat more clever at that sort of trick. If he took the cat's advice, it could hardly make things worse. So he did what the cat asked; and the cat pulled the boots on, slung the sack over his shoulder, and set off along the road.

He made for a field, went into the brambles at the edge of it and picked some thistles. The boots protected his feet from the sharp thorns. He put the thistles in the sack, and laid the sack down near the entrance to a rabbit burrow. The mouth of the sack was wide open. Then the cat stretched out on the ground as if he were dead.

In a moment or so, out of the burrow came a young rabbit. He caught sight of the thistles in the sack, and jumped in. In a flash the cat came to life; he pulled the cord at the mouth of the sack, and the rabbit was caught. Then off went the cat to the town, which was the biggest town in the country; and the biggest building in the town was the palace, where the king lived.

The sentry at the palace gate looked at the cat suspiciously. "Halt!" he cried. "What do you want, cat?"

The cat said, "You see this sack over my shoulder? In it there's a present for the king – a plump young rabbit."

"Oh," said the sentry. "Is there? Well, the king isn't in the habit of being visited by cats, even if they're bringing him presents."

"By ordinary cats, I guess not," said the cat. "But what about cats wearing fine boots, like these of mine?"

The sentry, who was not very bright, became confused. "Fine boots?" he said. "What's that got to do with it? Oh, well. All right, then. In you go. But I really don't know if it's the right thing to do . . ."

And while the sentry stood there, looking uneasy and

biting his lip, the cat slipped past him, and soon was standing before the king. The cat bowed low and laid the sack at the king's feet. "Your Majesty," he said, "this sack contains a very fine plump young rabbit. It is for you."

"Ah yes," said the king, who wasn't particularly bright either. "Oh. We thank you for it, cat."

"Oh don't thank me, Your Majesty," said the cat. "The gift is from my master, the Marquis of Carabas."

The king was more confused than the sentry had been. "Oh," he said. "The Marquis of Carabas, eh? Well, my young – er – friend, give your master the Marquis of Carabas our thanks and tell him that his present gives us the greatest pleasure."

So off went the cat, back to his master. But he told the young man nothing of what had happened.

The next day, off he went again. This time he lay down in a cornfield as if he were dead, leaving the sack on the ground full of thistles and with its mouth wide open. In no time two partridges had flown down straight into the sack. The cat came to life, pulled the strings in the mouth of the sack and trapped the birds inside. And off he went again to the palace. Once more he was halted by the sentry.

"Halt!" cried the sentry. "What's your . . .? Oh, it's you, is it, Master Cat?"

"It is, indeed," said the cat. "Today I have two plump partridges for the king."

"Two partridges!" cried the sentry. "What's that got to do with – Oh, very well, in you go. Though if it's the right thing to do, I . . ."

But the cat didn't wait to hear what the sentry had to say – which was just as well, because the sentry, now very confused, went on saying it for half an hour or more. Into the palace the cat went, and stood again before the king. He bowed low, and laid the sack at the king's feet.

"Your Majesty," he said, "this sack contains two fine plump partridges – for you!"

"And from your master again?" asked the king. "The Marquis of – er –"

"Of Carabas, Your Majesty," said the cat.

"Ah yes, yes, yes," said the king, who'd never heard of such a Marquis, but didn't like to say so. "Yes, a most excellent nobleman. Hmm – where do the partridges come from, Master Cat?"

"From my master's own hunting grounds, Your Majesty," said the cat. "His *vast* hunting grounds."

"Oh, quite," said the king. "Well, thank the Marquis for us, Master Cat. And for yourself, take these few pieces of gold."

"Your Majesty is too kind," said the cat.

"Not at all. Delighted," said the king. "Most generous of your master. Excellent nobleman. Marquis of –"

"Carabas, Your Majesty," said the cat.

"Marquis of Carabas, yes," said the king. "Yes, yes . . ."

But the cat didn't wait to hear the rest of what the king said – which was just as well, for the king went on muttering the name of the Marquis of Carabas, and saying he was an excellent nobleman, and wondering who on earth he was, for half an hour or more. But the cat bowed and left the room.

Back home, he again told his young master nothing of what had happened; but the few pieces of gold were enough to buy good meals for both of them.

And so it went on. Day after day, for two or three months, the cat took gifts to the king; and every time, he told the king that they had come from his master's hunting grounds. And every time the king said how grateful he was to this . . . Marquis of Carabas he had never met.

But one day the sentry told the cat that if he came with a gift for the king the following day, he would come in vain. "You see, Master Cat," said the sentry, who was now on very good terms with the cat, though he was still puzzled by the whole thing, "you see, tomorrow the king is going out for a long drive with his daughter. The loveliest princess in the world, Master Cat."

"Really?" said the cat, pricking up his ears. "Oh, *really*! Of course, their route – the way they're going on their drive – that's a secret, naturally?"

"Oh no, it's no secret," said the sentry. "They're going all the way along the river bank. You're looking very thoughtful, Master Cat."

"Oh," said the cat. "I was only thinking that . . . I must remember not to call at the palace tomorrow. Thank you, sentry. Good day."

And he hurried home purring to himself with delight and glee. He *had* been thinking – but it *wasn't* about not calling at the palace next day. As soon as he got home he cried, "Master! Master! If you follow my advice now, your fortune is made! All you have to do is to come with me tomorrow and bathe in the river. I'll do the rest."

You might have expected the miller's son to say he'd do nothing of the sort! Bathe in the river in order to come into a fortune! The cat must be mad! But by now the young man knew that, whatever was going on, he was master of perhaps the cleverest cat in the world. Well, what other cat had ever come home with gold to buy food with? So the miller's son said, "All right. I don't know what you're up to. But I'll do what you say."

"Good," said the cat. "There is one other small thing, master. If anyone should address you by some strange name

88

– the Marquis of Something–or–other, perhaps – don't look surprised. Whatever you do, *don't* look surprised! And *don't* say it isn't you!"

The miller's son laughed, a little uneasily. "Very well," he said. "But I hope these tricks of yours won't lead us into any trouble."

So next day the young man went with the cat down to the river. He undressed and plunged into the water to bathe. The cat went at once to a large stone on the river bank and hid something underneath it. At that moment came the sound of carriage wheels and horses' hooves, and the sound of horns. The king was coming, with the princess beside him in his golden carriage. The cat dashed onto the road and began shouting at the top of his voice, "Help! Help! My master is drowning! The Marquis of Carabas is drowning!"

The king looked out of the carriage and recognised the cat. At once he ordered the carriage to stop, and his guards to run to the river and save the Marquis. The guards leapt from their horses, rushed down to the water and pulled the cat's bewildered young master out of the water. Meanwhile the cat approached the carriage and, bowing deeply, said, "Oh, Your Majesty! Not only was my master drowning, but while he was in the water thieves came and made off with his clothes. Oh, what an unlucky day!"

"This is dreadful!" cried the king. "Quite dreadful! The Marquis must not go without clothes! Guard! Go at once to the palace and bring the finest suit from our wardrobe for My Lord the Marquis of Carabas! At the double!"

The truth is, of course, that the shabby clothes belonging to the cat's master had not been stolen. They were what the cat had hidden under that large stone.

The guard was soon back with a fine suit of clothes; and when the miller's son was dressed in these, he looked very handsome, and every inch a nobleman. The cat introduced him to the king. "Your Majesty – my master, the Marquis of Carabas!"

"My Lord Marquis," cried the king, "we are delighted to meet you at last. This is our daughter, the princess. And now, My Lord Marquis, it would give us the greatest pleasure if you would join us in the carriage and accompany us on our drive."

And with a blowing of horns and snorting of horses, and a fine sound of horses' hooves, off they went.

"But where, My Lord Marquis," said the king, "is that excellent servant of yours, the cat?"

"I – I think I see him, Your Majesty," said the miller's son. "He's hurrying ahead of us there in the distance." The young man, of course, had no idea what the cat was up to. So he said, "He has my orders, Your Majesty, and is busy carrying them out."

"Ah yes, indeed," said the king, and the carriage sped on. The miller's son shyly looked at the princess, and thought she was beautiful, and the princess shyly looked at the miller's son, and thought he was handsome.

Meanwhile, the cat was hurrying along the road well in front of the royal carriage. He came to a meadow that was being mowed, and hurried over to speak to the mowers.

"Good morning, my dear good mowers," he cried.

"Mornin', Master Cat," said the mowers.

"I have a message for you," said the cat. "The king is coming this way, and he's bound to ask you whose meadow you are mowing."

"Ah," said the mowers.

"You must reply," said the cat, "that the meadow belongs to My Lord the Marquis of Carabas. Can you remember that?"

"But – Master Cat . . .!" cried the mowers.

"I'm afraid," said the cat, "that if you don't do this it will be necessary to have you all chopped up into mincemeat."

"Into what?" cried the mowers.

"Oh! Mincemeat! Mincemeat! Mincemeat!" cried the cat, impatiently. "Surely you know what mincemeat is!"

"Ah, mincemeat," said the mowers. "Well, in that case, Master Cat, we will certainly do as you say. Marquis of –"

"Carabas," said the cat.

"Ah yes, Carabas," said the mowers. "Otherwise . . ."

"Mincemeat," said the cat.

"Ah yes," said the mowers. "We will do what you ask, Master Cat."

The cat hurried off, and the mowers went on with their work, trembling at the thought of what the cat had threatened. Soon they heard the sound of the royal carriage; and, as the cat had foreseen, it drew up beside the meadow. "This is a huge meadow you are mowing, my men," called the king. "To whom does this huge meadow belong?"

"Ah, Your Majesty, this huge meadow, Your Majesty, ah yes, Your Majesty," cried the mowers, feeling very anxious. "It belongs, Your Majesty, to the Marquis of – er – Carabas."

"The Marquis of Carabas!" cried the king, turning to the miller's son. "So it is your land, My Lord?"

"Ah yes, indeed," said the cat's master. He was becoming very confused, but he remembered what the cat had told him. He must say yes to everything. "Of course. I believe it is my land."

"Hmm," said the king. "Very fine land! Well, well . . . drive on . . ."

Meanwhile the cat had come to a cornfield that was being harvested. He bustled up to the harvesters.

"Good morning, my dear good harvesters," he cried.

"Mornin', Master Cat," said the harvesters.

"I bring you a message," said the cat. "The king is coming this way in his carriage. He is certain to ask whose cornfield this is that you are harvesting. I want you to reply that the cornfield belongs to My Lord the Marquis of Carabas. You understand?"

"But – Master Cat – !" cried the harvesters.

"Now, should you fail to do this," said the cat, briskly, "I should be forced, of course, to have you all chopped up into mincemeat."

"Into mincemeat, Master Cat?"

"That's what I said. Mincemeat!"

"Oh," said the harvesters, who hated the idea of being chopped up into mincemeat. "Oh, we'll tell the king, never you fear, Master Cat."

So the cat hurried off, and the harvesters went on with their work. A few moments later the royal carriage arrived, with a great sound of wheels and hooves and horns.

"Good morning, harvesters," called the king. "To whom does this splendid large field belong?"

"Ah, it belongs," said the harvesters, "er – to My Lord the Marquis of – Car – er – ab – er – as, Your Majesty. The Marquis of Carabas."

And as before, the king was astonished and delighted, and again he congratulated the miller's son on having such splendid fields. And so it went on. The cat always hurried ahead, and to all those he met he said the same thing: in cornfield and meadow, in pasture and by mill-stream, everywhere the cat gave his orders: and everywhere the king was told that this field or stream or mill belonged to the Marquis of Carabas.

And now the cat, hurrying ahead, had reached the foot of a high hill, on the top of which stood a large and splendid castle. There was an old woman coming down the hill, and the cat called to her. "Old woman, good day to you," he cried. "Tell me, who lives in the castle up there?"

"My master lives there," said the old woman. "Tell *me*, how far have you come, Master Cat?"

"I have come many miles along the river bank," said the cat. "Through many cornfields and meadows and pastures and by many mills."

"Well, everything you have seen on that journey," said the old woman, "belongs to my master. Of all the ogres in the world –"

"He's an ogre then, old woman?"

"Oh, he is indeed, a very wicked ogre. But as I was saying, of all the ogres in the world he is the richest. And he's the cleverest, too. He has the power of turning himself into any animal he has a mind to. Oh, he is clever – and terrible. Terrible, Master Cat!" And she cackled, as if it pleased her to think how terrible her master was.

"Well, thank you, old woman," said the cat thoughtfully: and he made his way up the hill to the great door of the castle. And there he tugged at the bell.

A servant opened the door, wearing a fine uniform. "What do you want, Master Cat?" he asked.

"I have come a long way to see your master and pay my respects to him," said the cat. "I would consider it the *greatest* honour to have a word or two with an ogre so *famous* and so *clever*. If you would repeat those words exactly to your master –"

A moment later the cat was shown into the great room where the ogre was sitting. "You wish," said the ogre, who was obviously pleased to have been told that the cat thought him famous and clever, "to have the honour of speaking to me, they tell me."

"Indeed, Master, that is an honour in itself," the cat replied. "But there is a greater honour that, alas, I can hardly hope for."

"And what is that?" asked the ogre.

"I have heard," said the cat, "that you have a remarkable power of changing yourself into all sorts of animals."

"That is so," said the ogre.

"Forgive me," said the cat, "but I can hardly believe it."

"I will prove it to you with the greatest of pleasure," said the delighted ogre. "Watch! I'll turn myself into –"

"May I suggest –" said the cat hastily.

"A lion!" said the ogre.

"A lion!" cried the cat. "Oh, my goodness! Oh yes, I see! So you are! I mean, so you have! I mean," said the cat, backing into the corner of the room, "I see you have turned yourself into a lion! Oh dear!"

"And back again to myself," said the ogre, to the cat's relief. "That gave you quite a fright, eh?"

"Ha ha!" said the cat, pretending to be amazed. "Yes, quite a fright! An astonishing trick! But I've heard that you can also turn yourself into a very small animal, like a rat . . . or a mouse . . . Now, that I do find hard to believe!

You are such a fine large ogre – I can't quite see how you could become anything so very small as a mouse."

"Why, that's easy! It's amazingly easy!" cried the ogre. "Just you watch!" And at once the immense ogre became a tiny mouse, scampering across the floor of the room. In a flash the cat was on him. Never in all his years at the mill had he sprung faster than he now sprang across the great floor of the ogre's room. One flash, one gulp, and the mouse had gone.

And at that very moment came a sound from the roadway outside the castle: wheels, hooves, horns. The royal carriage had arrived. It drew to a halt outside the door of the castle. Then came the sound of the bell. At once the cat flashed along the great corridors, drew the bolt of the huge door and swung it open. Out he ran and bowed low to the king.

"Welcome, Your Majesty," he cried, "to the castle."

"Why," cried the king, turning to the miller's son. "This is your cat, your servant, My Lord Marquis."

If the miller's son had not been wearing a fine feathered hat from the king's wardrobe, his hair would have stood on end. He didn't know *what* was going on! But he managed to say, "Ah yes, it is, Your Majesty. Indeed, that is my servant, the cat."

"Who else should it be," said the cat, who looked as pleased as if he'd just swallowed a mouse (which, of course, he had), "since this is the castle of My Lord the Marquis of Carabas."

"What, My Lord!" cried the king. "This great castle is yours, too? Let's go inside at once!"

And in they went, up great stone steps to a fine hall. There, a magnificent feast was waiting for them. Actually, it had been prepared by the ogre for some of his friends who were to visit him that day: but as they approached the castle they'd seen the King's carriage standing before it, and had not dared to come in.

The cat bowed low and said, "Your Majesty, you see now why I ran ahead of your carriage. It was so that I might reach the castle first and have this feast prepared for you and the princess and my master."

And so the feasting began. The king sat at the head of

the table, and the cat gave orders to the ogre's servants, who brought in the food and the wine. The servants said nothing, then or ever after, about the ogre, for the cat had commanded them to be silent. What threat he used, I can't say for certain, though I believe the word mincemeat came into it. And that is almost all of this story, except that the king made a speech.

"Hem – er – my friends," he began. "I have been – er – quite astonished today by what I have seen of the – er – vast lands and possessions of the Marquis of Carabas. Now, I think it would be safe, My Lord Marquis, to say (for I've been watching you both in the carriage) that you admire my daughter: and just as safe, I'm sure, to say that – er – she greatly admires you. In short, you have but to say the word, and – er – the hand of the princess in marriage is yours."

And so it was. On that very same day the miller's son who had become the Marquis of Carabas was married to the king's daughter, and so became a prince.

And that, I think, is the whole story. Oh yes, the cat. He was made, by his grateful master, a lord himself – not quite a marquis, but very nearly. From then on he hunted mice only now and then, for fun. And, as befitted a great lord, he wore boots for the rest of his life.

RABBIT AND THE WOLVES

Ruth Manning-Sanders

Rabbit's grandmother had given him a little pipe. Now he was skipping along through the woods, *lipperty-lipperty-lip-lip-lipperty*, and playing on his little flute. Rabbit didn't live in the woods himself. He lived in Grandmother's house; but he had lots of friends in the woods, and his best friend of all was Marmot, who lived in a hole under a tree stump. Now Rabbit was going to show his new pipe to Marmot. He was looking forward to showing the pipe to his best friend, Marmot.

So on frisked Rabbit, *lipperty-lipperty-lip-lip-lipperty* . . . and then, oh dear, what do you think? Out from behind the trees jumped seven great wolves.

"Rabbit, we're going to eat you!"

Rabbit was a brave little fellow. If he was frightened, he wasn't going to show it. He said, "Well, I own you've caught me fairly. But, dear me, you can't *all* eat me, you know; I'm only a mouthful. Well, which of you is it to be?"

The Wolves began to quarrel then, because they all wanted to eat Rabbit. But Rabbit said, "Don't quarrel! Don't quarrel! I've got a good idea. Do you like dancing?"

"Of course we do! Of course we do!" cried the Wolves.

"Well then," said Rabbit, "I know a lovely new dance,

and I was just longing to teach it to someone. Shall I teach it to you? Then the one who dances best can have me for a prize."

The Wolves agreed that it *was* a good idea. So Rabbit said, "This dance is in seven parts. For the first part, you get into line, one behind the other. I lean against this tree, and when I begin to sing, you all dance away from me. When I stop singing and call out '*Hu!*' then you dance back. But you must keep in line, and dance properly; no floundering about."

"No, no! No floundering about!" cried the Wolves.

So Rabbit leaned against a tree and began to sing:

> "Ha, how tasty,
> Ha, how toothsome,
> Ha, how tender,
> Little Rabbit flesh!"

And the Wolves danced away from him, keeping in line, one behind the other, and lifting their feet to the time of his singing.

"*Hu!*" cried Rabbit, when they had danced some way. And the Wolves swung round and came dancing back to him. "Keep in line, keep in line!" cried Rabbit. "Lift your feet neatly! Ah, that's very good . . . Yes, that was really charming!" he said, as the Wolves gathered round him.

"Now," said he, "we come to the second part of the dance. I go to that tree over there, and you form

in line again. I sing, you dance away, and when I call 'Hu!'
you turn and come dancing back. This second part of the
dance is very like the first, only at every fourth step you
fling back your heads and give a nice little howl. Got that?"

"Yes, yes," cried the Wolves. "This is great fun!"

So Rabbit went and leaned against this other tree, and
began to sing again:

> "Ha, how tasty,
> Ha, how toothsome,
> Ha, how tender,
> Little Rabbit flesh!"

And the Wolves danced away, keeping in line, one
behind the other, lifting their feet, and at every fourth step
flinging back their heads and howling. It would have been
the funniest sight in the world, if only Rabbit had felt more

like laughing. But he didn't feel like laughing, you may be sure.

So, when the Wolves had danced quite a long way, he called out "*Hu!*" and the Wolves all turned and came dancing back.

"Well now, that was even better than the first time," said Rabbit. "In all my life I've never seen such beautiful dancing!" And he went on to a third tree. "For this third part of the dance you do a polka," said he. "Do you know the polka step?"

"Of course we do!" cried the Wolves.

"Well then, off you go!" said Rabbit. And he began to sing, "*One* and *two* and *three* and *four! Hop* and *hop* and *hop* and *hop!*"

Off went the Wolves, hopping and skipping. They were laughing like anything. They were enjoying themselves so much that they had almost forgotten about eating Rabbit. Though of course Rabbit knew they would remember it again as soon as the dance ended.

"*Hu!*" he called once more, and all the Wolves came polka-ing back. "Magnificent!" said Rabbit, moving to a fourth tree.

And what do you think cunning little Rabbit was doing, as he moved from tree to tree? Just this: with every tree he came to, he was getting nearer and nearer to the hole under the tree stump where his best friend, Marmot, lived.

So he sent the Wolves off in a fourth dance and a fifth dance, and a sixth dance, and between every dance he moved on to another tree, nearer to Marmot's hole.

"*Hu!*" he cried for the sixth time. And the Wolves came dancing back. They were really proud of themselves.

And Rabbit moved to yet another tree.

"Now this is the seventh and last part of the dance," said he. "It's called the Sun dance, and it's a gallop. You go as fast as you can, and at every seventh step you turn a somersault. Understand? Well then, get ready to go. I'll count three, and then you start. But remember as soon as I shout '*Hu!*' you all turn round and come racing back. And then – oh dear! – the first that reaches me gobbles me up. . . . Well, of course," he added, wiping his eyes, "one can't live for ever. But seeing you dance so beautifully has made my last moments happy . . . One, two, *three*!" he shouted, and off galloped the Wolves.

"Dance away, Wolves, dance away!
See us dancing, dancing, dancing!
We dance, we dance, we dance the Sun dance,
See how beautifully we dance!"

sang Rabbit.

"Dance away now, dance away!" shouted the Wolves, turning a somersault at every seventh step. "See how beautifully we dance!"

"Hurrah!" cried Rabbit.

"*Hurrah! Hurrah! Hurrah!*" shouted the Wolves. Their voices were getting fainter and fainter. They were a long way off now. Rabbit could only just see their grey bodies flickering in and out among the trees. But something else he could see, quite close to him, and that was the tree stump where Marmot had her hole. And, bless me, if that wasn't Marmot's little anxious face, peeping out at him!

"*Hu!*" shouted Rabbit – and made a dash for the hole.

The Wolves turned and came racing back, each one determined to be first, that he might gobble up Rabbit. But what did they see when they came back to the starting place? Nothing at all!

Only from under the ground nearby they heard Rabbit singing:

"Dance away now, dance away,
Dance away, Wolves, dance away!
But you won't eat Rabbit, not today,
Not today, Wolves, not today!"

THE TALE OF THE SILVER SAUCER AND THE TRANSPARENT APPLE

Arthur Ransome

There was once an old peasant, and he must have had more brains under his hair than ever I had, for he was a merchant, and used to take things every year to sell at the big fair of Nijni Novgorod. Well, I could never do that. I could never have been anything better than an old forester.

"Never mind, grandfather," said Maroosia.

God knows best, and He makes some merchants and some foresters, and some good and some bad, all in His own way. Anyhow, this one was a merchant, and he had three daughters. There were none of them so bad to look at, but one of them was as pretty as Maroosia. And she was the best of them too. The others put all the hard work on her, while they did nothing but look at themselves in the looking-glass and complain of what they had to eat. They called the pretty one "Little Stupid", because she was so good and did all their work for them. Oh, they were real bad ones, those two. We wouldn't have them in here for a minute.

Well, the time came round for the merchant to pack up and go to the big fair. He called his daughters, and said, "Little pigeons", just as I say to you. "Little pigeons," says he, "what would you like me to bring you from the fair?"

Says the eldest, "I'd like a necklace but it must be a very rich one."

Says the second, "I want a new dress with gold hems."

But the youngest, the good one, Little Stupid, said nothing at all.

"Now little one," says her father, "what is it you want? I must bring something for you too."

Says the little one, "Could I have a silver saucer and a transparent apple? But never mind if there are none."

The old merchant says, "Long hair, short sense," just as I say to Maroosia; but he promised the little pretty one, who was so good that her sisters called her stupid, that if he could get her a silver saucer and a transparent apple she should have them.

Then they all kissed each other, and he cracked his whip, and off he went, with the little bells jingling on the horses' harness.

The three sisters waited till he came back. The two elder ones looked in the looking-glass, and thought how fine they would look in the new necklace and the new dress; but the little pretty one took care of her old mother, and scrubbed and washed and dusted and swept and cooked, and every day the other two complained that the soup was burnt or the bread not properly baked.

Then one day there was a jingling of bells and a clattering of horses' hoofs, and the old merchant came driving back from the fair.

The sisters ran out.

"Where is the necklace?" asked the first.

"You haven't forgotten the dress?" asked the second.

But the little one, Little Stupid, helped her old father off with his coat, and asked him if he was tired.

"Well, little one," says the old merchant, "and don't you want your fairing too? I went from one end of the market to the other before I could get what you wanted. I bought the silver saucer from an old Jew, and the transparent apple from a Finnish hag."

"Oh, thank you, father," says the little one.

"And what will you do with them?" says he.

"I shall spin the apple in the saucer," says the little pretty one, and at that the old merchant burst out laughing.

"They don't call you 'Little Stupid' for nothing," says he.

Well, they all had their fairings, and the two elder sisters, the bad ones, they ran off and put on the new dress and the new necklace, and came out and strutted about, preening themselves like herons, now on one leg and now on the other, to see how they looked. But Little Stupid, she just sat herself down beside the stove, and took the transparent apple and set it in the silver saucer, and she laughed softly to herself. And then she began spinning the apple in the saucer.

Round and round the apple spun in the saucer, faster and faster, till you couldn't see the apple at all, nothing but a mist like a little whirlpool in the silver saucer. And the little good one looked at it, and her eyes shone like yours.

Her sisters laughed at her.

"Spinning an apple in a saucer and staring at it, the little stupid," they said, as they strutted about the room, listening to the rustle of the new dress and fingering the bright round stones of the necklace.

But the little pretty one did not mind them. She sat in the corner watching the spinning apple. And as it spun she talked to it.

"Spin, spin, apple in the silver saucer." This is what she said. "Spin so that I may see the world. Let me have a peep at the little father Tsar on his high throne. Let me see the rivers and the ships and the great towns far away."

And as she looked at the little glass whirlpool in the saucer, there was the Tsar, the little father – God preserve him! – sitting on his high throne. Ships sailed on the seas, their white sails swelling in the wind. There was Moscow with its white stone walls and painted churches. Why, there were the market at Nijni Novgorod, and the Arab merchants with their camels, and the Chinese with their

blue trousers and bamboo staves. And then there was the great river Volga, with men on the banks towing ships against the stream. Yes, and she saw a sturgeon asleep in a deep pool.

"Oh! oh! oh!" says the little pretty one, as she saw all these things.

And the bad ones, they saw how her eyes shone, and they came and looked over her shoulder, and saw how all the world was there, in the spinning apple and the silver saucer. And the old father came and looked over her shoulder too, and he saw the market at Nijni Novgorod.

"Why, there is the inn where I put up the horses," says he. "You haven't done so badly after all, Little Stupid."

And the little pretty one, Little Stupid, went on staring into the glass whirlpool in the saucer, spinning the apple, and seeing all the world she had never seen before, floating there before her in the saucer, brighter than leaves in sunlight.

The bad ones, the elder sisters, were sick with envy.

"Little Stupid," says the first, "if you will give me your silver saucer and your transparent apple, I will give you my fine new necklace."

"Little Stupid," says the second, "I will give you my new dress with gold hems if you will give me your transparent apple and your silver saucer."

"Oh, I couldn't do that," says the Little Stupid, and she goes on spinning the apple in the saucer and seeing what was happening all over the world.

So the bad ones put their wicked heads together and thought of a plan. And they took their father's axe, and went into the deep forest and hid it under a bush.

The next day they waited till afternoon, when work was done, and the little pretty one was spinning her apple in the saucer. They said –

"Come along, Little Stupid; we are all going to gather berries in the forest."

"Do you really want me to come too?" says the little one. She would rather have played with her apple and saucer.

But they said, "Why, of course. You don't think we can carry all the berries ourselves!"

So the little one jumped up, and found the baskets, and went with them to the forest. But before she started she ran

to her father, who was counting his money, and was not too pleased to be interrupted, for figures go quickly out of your head when you have a lot of them to remember. She asked him to take care of the silver saucer and the transparent apple for fear she would lose them in the forest.

"Very well, little bird," says the old man, and he put the things in a box with a lock and key to it. He was a merchant, you know, and that sort are always careful about things, and go clattering about with a lot of keys at their belt. I've nothing to lock up, and never had, and perhaps it is just as well, for I could never be bothered with keys.

So the little one picks up all three baskets and runs off after the others, the bad ones, with black hearts under their necklaces and new dresses.

They went deep into the forest, picking berries, and the little one picked so fast that she soon had a basket full. She was picking and picking, and did not see what the bad ones were doing. They were fetching the axe.

The little one stood up to straighten her back, which ached after so much stooping, and she saw her two sisters standing in front of her, looking at her cruelly. Their

baskets lay on the ground quite empty. They had not picked a berry. The eldest had the axe in her hand.

The little one was frightened.

"What is it, sisters?" says she; "and why do you look at me with cruel eyes? And what is the axe for? You are not going to cut berries with an axe."

"No, Little Stupid," says the first, "we are not going to cut berries with the axe."

"No, Little Stupid," says the second; "the axe is here for something else."

The little one begged them not to frighten her.

Says the first, "Give me your transparent apple."

Says the second, "Give me your silver saucer."

"If you don't give them up at once, we shall kill you." That is what the bad ones said.

The poor little one begged them. "O sisters, do not kill me! I haven't got the saucer or the apple with me at all."

"What a lie!" say the bad ones. "You never would leave it behind."

And one caught her by the hair, and the other swung the axe, and between them they killed the pretty little one, who was called Little Stupid because she was so good.

Then they looked for the saucer and the apple, and could not find them. But it was too late now. So they made a hole in the ground, and buried the little one under a birch tree.

When the sun went down the bad ones came home, and they wailed with false voices, and rubbed their eyes to make the tears come. They made their eyes red and their noses too, and they did not look any prettier for that.

"What is the matter with you, little pigeons?" said the old merchant and his wife. I would not say "little pigeons" to such bad ones. Black-hearted crows I would call them.

And they wail and lament aloud —

"We are miserable for ever. Our poor little sister is lost. We looked for her everywhere. We heard the wolves howling. They must have eaten her."

The old mother and father cried like rivers in springtime, because they loved the little pretty one, who was called Little Stupid because she was so good.

But before their tears were dry the bad ones began to ask for the silver saucer and the transparent apple.

"No, no," says the old man; "I shall keep them for ever, in memory of my poor little daughter whom God has taken away."

So the bad ones did not gain by killing their little sister.

"That is one good thing," said Vanya.

"But is that all, grandfather?" said Maroosia.

"Wait a bit, little pigeons. Too much haste set his shoes on fire. You listen, and you will hear what happened," said old Peter. He took a pinch of snuff from a little wooden box, and then he went on with his tale.

Time did not stop with the death of the little girl. Winter came, and the snow with it. Everything was white, just as it is now. And the wolves came to the doors of the huts, even into the villages, and no one stirred farther than he need. And then the snow melted, and the buds broke on the trees, and the birds began singing, and the sun shone warmer every day. The old people had almost forgotten the little pretty one who lay dead in the forest. The bad ones had not forgotten, because now they had to do the work, and they did not like that at all.

And then one day some lambs strayed away into the forest, and a young shepherd went after them to bring them safely back to their mothers. And as he wandered this way and that through the forest, following their light tracks, he came to a little birch tree, bright with new leaves, waving over a little mound of earth. And there was a reed growing in the mound, and that, you know as well as I, is a strange thing, one reed all by itself under a birch tree in the forest. But it was no stranger than the flowers, for there were flowers round it, some red as the sun at dawn and others blue as the summer sky.

Well, the shepherd looks at the reed, and he looks at those flowers, and he thinks, "I've never seen anything like that before. I'll make a whistle-pipe of that reed, and keep it for a memory till I grow old."

So he did. He cut the reed, and sat himself down on the mound, and carved away at the reed with his knife, and got the pith out of it by pushing a twig through it, and beating it gently till the bark swelled, made holes in it, and there was his whistle-pipe. And then he put it to his lips to see what sort of music he could make on it. But that he never knew, for before his lips touched it the whistle-pipe began

115

playing by itself and reciting in a girl's sweet voice. This is what it sang:

"Play, play, whistle-pipe. Bring happiness to my dear father and to my little mother. I was killed – yes, my life was taken from me in the deep forest for the sake of a silver saucer, for the sake of a transparent apple."

When he heard that the shepherd went back quickly to the village to show it to the people. And all the way the whistle-pipe went on playing and reciting, singing its little song. And every one who heard it said, "What a strange song! But who is it who was killed?"

"I know nothing about it," says the shepherd, and he tells them about the mound and the reed and the flowers, and how he cut the reed and made the whistle-pipe, and how the whistle-pipe does its playing by itself.

And as he was going through the village, with all the people crowding about him, the old merchant, that one who was the father of the two bad ones and of the little pretty one, came along and listened with the rest. And when he heard the words about the silver saucer and the transparent apple, he snatched the whistle-pipe from the shepherd boy. And still it sang:

"Play, play, whistle-pipe! Bring happiness to my dear father and to my little mother. I was killed – yes, for my life was taken from me in the deep forest for the sake of a silver saucer, for the sake of a transparent apple."

And the old merchant remembered the little good one, and his tears trickled over his cheeks and down his old beard. Old men love little pigeons, you know. And he said to the shepherd –

"Take me at once to the mound, where you say you cut the reed."

The shepherd led the way, and the old man walked beside him, crying, while the whistle-pipe in his hand went on singing and reciting its little song over and over again.

They came to the mound under the birch tree, and there were the flowers, shining red and blue, and there in the middle of the mound was the stump of the reed which the shepherd had cut.

The whistle-pipe sang on and on.

Well, there and then they dug up the mound, and there was the little girl lying under the dark earth as if she were fast asleep.

"O God of mine," says the old merchant, "this is my daughter, my little pretty one, whom we called Little Stupid." He began to weep loudly and wring his hands; but the whistle-pipe, playing and reciting, changed its song. This is what it sang:

"My sisters took me into the forest to look for the red berries. In the deep forest they killed poor me for the sake of a silver saucer, for the sake of a transparent apple. Wake me, dear father, from a bitter dream, by fetching water from the well of the Tsar."

How the people scowled at the two sisters! They scowled, they cursed them for the bad ones they were. And the bad ones, the two sisters, wept, and fell on their knees, and confessed everything. They were taken, and their hands were tied, and they were shut up in prison.

"Do not kill them," begged the old merchant, "for then I should have no daughters at all, and when there are no fish in the river we make shift with crays. Besides, let me go to the Tsar and beg water from his well. Perhaps my little daughter will wake up, as the whistle-pipe tells us."

And the whistle-pipe sang again:

"Wake me, wake me, dear father, from a bitter dream, by fetching water from the well of the Tsar. Till then, dear father, a blanket of black earth and the shade of the green birch tree."

So they covered the little girl with her blanket of earth, and the shepherd with his dogs watched the mound night and day. He begged for the whistle-pipe to keep him company, poor lad, and all the days and nights he thought of the sweet face of the little pretty one he had seen there under the birch tree.

The old merchant harnessed his horse, as if he were going to the town; and he drove off through the forest, along the roads, till he came to the palace of the Tsar, the little father of all good Russians. And then he left his horse and cart and waited on the steps of the palace.

The Tsar, the little father, with rings on his fingers and a gold crown on his head, came out on the steps in the morning sunshine; and as for the old merchant, he fell on his knees and kissed the feet of the Tsar, and begged –

118

"O little father, Tsar, give me leave to take water – just a little drop of water – from your holy well."

"And what will you do with it?" says the Tsar.

"I will wake my daughter from a bitter dream," says the old merchant. "She was murdered by her sisters – killed in the deep forest – for the sake of a silver saucer, for the sake of a transparent apple."

"A silver saucer?" says the Tsar – "a transparent apple? Tell me about that."

And the old merchant told the Tsar everything, just as I have told it to you.

And the Tsar, the little father, he gave the old merchant a glass of water from his holy well. "But," says he, "when your daughterkin wakes, bring her to me, and her sisters with her, and also the silver saucer and the transparent apple."

The old man kissed the ground before the Tsar, and took the glass of water and drove home with it, and I can tell you he was careful not to spill a drop. He carried it all the way

119

in one hand as he drove.

He came to the forest and to the flowering mound under the little birch tree, and there was the shepherd watching with his dogs. The old merchant and the shepherd took away the blanket of black earth. Tenderly, the shepherd used his fingers, until the little girl, the pretty one, the good one, lay there as sweet as if she were not dead.

Then the merchant scattered the holy water from the glass over the little girl. And his daughterkin blushed as she lay there, and opened her eyes, and passed a hand across them, as if she were waking from a dream. And then she leapt up, crying and laughing, and clung about her old father's neck. And there they stood, the two of them, laughing and crying with joy. And the shepherd could not take his eyes from her, and in his eyes there were tears.

But the old father did not forget what he had promised the Tsar. He set the little pretty one, who had been so good that her wicked sisters had called her Stupid, to sit beside him on the cart. And he brought something from the house in a coffer of wood, and kept it under his coat. And they brought out the two sisters, the bad ones, from their dark prison, and set them in the cart. And the Little Stupid

kissed them and cried over them, and wanted to loose their hands, but the old merchant would not let her. And they all drove together till they came to the palace of the Tsar. The shepherd boy could not take his eyes from the little pretty one, and he ran all the way behind the cart.

Well, they came to the palace, and waited on the steps; and the Tsar came out to take the morning air, and he saw the old merchant, and the two sisters with their hands tied, and the little pretty one, as lovely as a spring day. And the Tsar saw her, and could not take his eyes from her. He did not see the shepherd boy, who hid away among the crowd.

Says the great Tsar to his soldiers, pointing to the bad sisters, "These two are to be put to death at sunset. When the sun goes down their heads must come off, for they are not fit to see another day."

Then he turns to the little pretty one, and he says: "Little sweet pigeon, where is your silver saucer, and where is your transparent apple?"

The old merchant took the wooden box from under his coat, and opened it with a key at his belt, and gave it to the little one, and she took out the silver saucer and the transparent apple and gave them to the Tsar.

"O lord Tsar," says she, "spin the apple in the saucer, and you will see whatever you wish to see – your soldiers, your high hills, your forests, your plains, your rivers, and everything in all Russia." And the Tsar, the little father, spun the apple in the saucer till it seemed a little whirlpool of white mist, and there he saw glittering towns, and regiments of soldiers marching to war, and ships, and day and night, and the clear stars above the trees. He looked at these things and thought much of them.

Then the little good one threw herself on her knees

before him, weeping.

"O little father, Tsar," she says, "take my transparent apple and my silver saucer; only forgive my sisters. Do not kill them because of me. If their heads are cut off when the sun goes down, it would have been better for me to lie under the blanket of black earth in the shade of the birch tree in the forest."

The Tsar was pleased with the kind heart of the little pretty one, and he forgave the bad ones, and their hands were untied, and the little pretty one kissed them, and they kissed her again and said they were sorry.

The old merchant looked up at the sun, and saw how the time was going.

"Well, well," says he, "it's time we were getting ready to go home."

They all fell on their knees before the Tsar and thanked him. But the Tsar could not take his eyes from the little pretty one, and would not let her go.

"Little sweet pigeon," says he, "will you be my Tsaritza, and a kind mother to Holy Russia?"

And the little good one did not know what to say. She blushed and answered, very rightly, "As my father orders, and as my little mother wishes, so shall it be."

The Tsar was pleased with her answer, and he sent a messenger on a galloping horse to ask leave from the little pretty one's old mother. And of course the old mother said that she was more than willing. So that was all right. Then there was a wedding – such a wedding! – and every city in Russia sent a silver plate of bread, and a golden salt-cellar, with their good wishes to the Tsar and Tsaritza.

Only the shepherd boy, when he heard that the little pretty one was to marry the Tsar, turned sadly away.

"Are you happy, little sweet pigeon?" says the Tsar.

"Oh yes," says the Little Stupid, who was now Tsaritza and mother of Holy Russia; "but there is one thing that would make me happier."

"And what is that?" says the lord Tsar.

"I cannot bear to lose my old father and my little mother and my dear sisters. Let them be with me here in the palace, as they were in my father's house."

The Tsar laughed at the little pretty one, but he agreed, and the little pretty one ran to tell them the good news. She said to her sisters, "Let all be forgotten, and all be forgiven, and may the evil eye fall on the one who first speaks of what has been!"

For a long time the Tsar lived, and the little pretty one the Tsaritza, and they had many children, and were very happy together. And ever since then the Tsars of Russia have kept the silver saucer and the transparent apple, so that, whenever they wish, they can see everything that is going on all over Russia. Perhaps even now the Tsar, the little father – God preserve him! – is spinning the apple in the saucer, and looking at us, and thinking it is time that two little pigeons were in bed.

"Is that the end?" said Vanya.

"That is the end," said old Peter.

"Poor shepherd boy!" said Maroosia.

"I don't know about that," said old Peter. "You see, if he had married the little pretty one, and had to have all the family to live with him, he would have had them in a hut like ours instead of in a great palace, and so he would never have had room to get away from them. And now, little pigeons, who is going to be first into bed?"

THE SING-SONG OF OLD MAN KANGAROO

Rudyard Kipling

Not always was the Kangaroo as now we do behold him, but a Different Animal with four short legs. He was grey and he was woolly, and his pride was inordinate: he danced on an outcrop in the middle of Australia, and he went to the Little God Nqa.

He went to Nqa at six before breakfast, saying, "Make me different from all other animals by five this afternoon."

Up jumped Nqa from his seat on the sand-flat and shouted, "Go away!"

He was grey and he was woolly, and his pride was inordinate: he danced on a rock-ledge in the middle of Australia, and he went to the Middle God Nquing.

He went to Nquing at eight after breakfast, saying, "Make me different from all other animals; make me, also, wonderfully popular by five this afternoon."

Up jumped Nquing from his burrow in the spinifex and shouted, "Go away!"

He was grey and he was woolly, and his pride was inordinate: he danced on a sandbank in the middle of Australia, and he went to the Big God Nqong.

He went to Nqong at ten before dinner-time, saying, "Make me different from all other animals; make me popular and wonderfully run after by five this afternoon."

Up jumped Nqong from his bath in the salt-pan and shouted, "Yes, I will!"

Nqong called Dingo – Yellow-Dog Dingo – always hungry, dusty in the sunshine, and showed him Kangaroo. Nqong said, "Dingo! Wake up, Dingo! Do you see that gentleman dancing on an ashpit? He wants to be popular and very truly run after. Dingo, make him so!"

Up jumped Dingo – Yellow-Dog Dingo – and said, "What, *that* cat-rabbit?"

Off ran Dingo – Yellow-Dog Dingo – always hungry, grinning like a coal-scuttle – ran after Kangaroo.

Off went the proud Kangaroo on his four little legs like a bunny.

This, O Beloved of mine, ends the first part of the tale!

He ran through the desert; he ran through the mountains; he ran through the salt-pans; he ran through the reed-beds; he ran through the blue gums; he ran through the spinifex; he ran till his front legs ached.

He had to!

Still ran Dingo – Yellow-Dog Dingo – always hungry, grinning like a rat-trap, never getting nearer, never getting farther – ran after Kangaroo.

He had to!

Still ran Kangaroo – Old Man Kangaroo. He ran through the ti-trees; he ran through the mulga; he ran through the long grass; he ran through the short grass; he ran through the Tropics of Capricorn and Cancer; he ran till his hind legs ached.

He had to!

Still ran Dingo – Yellow-Dog Dingo – always hungry, grinning like a horse-collar, never getting nearer, never getting farther; and they came to the Wollgong River.

Now, there wasn't any bridge, and there wasn't any ferry-boat, and Kangaroo didn't know how to get over; so he stood on his legs and hopped.

He had to!

He hopped through the Flinders; he hopped through the Cinders; he hopped through the deserts in the middle of Australia. He hopped like a Kangaroo.

First he hopped one yard; then he hopped three yards; then he hopped five yards; his legs growing stronger; his legs growing longer. He hadn't any time for rest or refreshment, and he wanted them very much.

Still ran Dingo – Yellow-Dog Dingo – very much bewildered, very much hungry, and wondering what in the world or out of it made Old Man Kangaroo hop.

For he hopped like a cricket; like a pea in a saucepan; or a new rubber ball on a nursery floor.

He had to!

He tucked up his front legs; he hopped on his hind legs; he stuck out his tail for a balance-weight behind him; and he hopped through the Darling Downs.

He had to!

Still ran Dingo – Tired-Dog Dingo – hungrier and hungrier, very much bewildered, and wondering when in the world or out of it would Old Man Kangaroo stop.

Then came Nqong from his bath in the salt-pans, and said, "It's five o'clock."

Down sat Dingo – Poor-Dog Dingo – always hungry, dusty in the sunshine; hung out his tongue and howled.

Down sat Kangaroo – Old Man Kangaroo – stuck out his tail like a milking-stool behind him, and said, "Thank goodness *that's* finished!"

Then said Nqong, who is always a gentleman, "Why aren't you grateful to Yellow-Dog Dingo? Why don't you thank him for all he has done for you?"

Then said Kangaroo – Tired Old Kangaroo – "He's chased me from the homes of my childhood; he's chased me out of my regular meal-times; he's altered my shape so I'll never get it back; and he's played Old Scratch with my legs."

Then said Nqong, "Perhaps I'm mistaken, but didn't you ask me to make you different from all other animals, and to make you very truly sought after? And now it is five o'clock."

"Yes," said Kangaroo. "I wish that I hadn't. I thought you would do it by charms and incantations, but this is a practical joke."

"Joke!" said Nqong, from his bath in the blue gums. "Say that again and I'll call up Dingo to run your hind legs off."

"No," said the Kangaroo. "I must apologise. Legs are legs, and you needn't alter 'em so far as I am concerned. I only meant to explain to Your Lordliness that I've had nothing to eat since morning, and I'm very empty indeed."

"Yes," said Dingo – Yellow-Dog Dingo – "I am just in the same situation. I've made him different from all other animals; but what may I have for my tea?"

Then said Nqong from his bath in the salt-pan, "Come and ask me about it tomorrow, because I'm going to wash."

So they were left in the middle of Australia, Old Man Kangaroo and Yellow-Dog Dingo, and each said, "That's *your* fault."

THE FAIRY SHIP

Alison Uttley

Little Tom was the son of a sailor. He lived in a small whitewashed cottage in Cornwall, on the rocky cliffs looking over the sea. From his bedroom window he could watch the great waves with their curling plumes of white foam, and count the seagulls as they circled in the blue sky. The water went right away to the dim horizon, and sometimes Tom could see the smoke from ships like a dark flag in the distance. Then he ran to get his spy-glass, to get a better view.

Tom's father was somewhere out on that great stretch of ocean, and all Tom's thoughts were there, following him, wishing for him to come home. Every day he ran down the narrow path to the small rocky bay, and sat there waiting for the ship to return. It was no use to tell him that a ship could not enter the tiny cove with its sharp needles or rocks and dangerous crags. Tom was certain that he would see his sailor father step out to the strip of sand if he kept watch. It seemed the proper way to come home.

December brought wild winds that swept the coast. Little Tom was kept indoors, for the gales would have blown him away like a gull's feather if he had gone to the rocky pathway. He was deeply disappointed that he couldn't keep watch in his favourite place. A letter had come, saying that his father was on his way home and any time he might arrive. Tom feared he wouldn't be there to see him, and he stood by the window for hours, watching the sky and the wild tossing sea.

"What shall I have for Christmas, Mother?" he asked one day. "Will Father Christmas remember to bring me something?"

"Perhaps he will, if our ship comes home in time," smiled his mother, and then she sighed and looked out at the wintry scene.

"Will he come in a sleigh with eight reindeer pulling it?" persisted Tom.

"Maybe he will," said his mother, but she wasn't thinking what she was saying. Tom knew at once, and he pulled her skirt.

"Mother! I don't think so, I don't think he will," said he.

"Will what, Tom? What are you talking about?"

"Father Christmas won't come in a sleigh, because there isn't any snow here. Besides, it is too rocky, and the reindeer would slip. I think he'll come in a ship, a grand ship with blue sails and a gold mast."

Little Tom took a deep breath and his eyes shone.

"Don't you think so, Mother? Blue sails, or maybe red ones. Satin like our parlour cushion. My father will come back with him. He'll come in a ship full of presents, and Father Christmas will give him some for me."

Tom's mother suddenly laughed aloud.

"Of course he will, little Tom. Father Christmas comes in a sleigh drawn by a team of reindeer to the children of towns and villages, but to the children of the sea he sails in a ship with all the presents tucked away in the hold."

She took her little son up in her arms and kissed him, but he struggled away and went back to the window.

"I'm going to be a sailor soon," he announced proudly. "Soon I shall be big enough, and then I shall go over the sea."

He looked out at the stormy sea where his father was sailing, every day coming nearer home, and on that wild water he saw only mist and spray, and the cruel waves dashing over the jagged splinters of rock.

Christmas morning came, and it was a day of surprising sunshine and calm. The seas must have known it was Christmas and they kept peace and goodwill. They danced into the cove in sparkling waves, and fluttered their flags of white foam, and tossed their treasures of seaweed and shells on the narrow beach.

Tom awoke early, and looked in his stocking on the bed-post. There was nothing in it at all! He wasn't surprised. Land children had their presents dropped down the chimney, but he, a sailor's son, had to wait for the ship. The stormy weather had kept the Christmas ship at sea, but now she was bound to come.

His mother's face was happy and excited, as if she had a secret. Her eyes shone with joy, and she seemed to dance round the room in excitement, but she said nothing.

Tom ate his breakfast quietly – a bantam egg and some honey for a special treat. Then he ran outside, to the gate, and down the slippery grassy path which led to the sea.

"Where are you going, Tom?" called his mother. "You wait here, and you'll see something."

"No, Mother. I'm going to look for the ship, the little Christmas ship," he answered, and away he trotted, so his mother turned to the house, and made her own preparations for the man she loved. The tide was out and it was safe now the winds had dropped.

She looked through the window, and she could see the little boy sitting on a rock on the sand, staring away at the sea. His gold hair was blown back, his blue jersey was wrinkled about his stout little body. The gulls swooped round him as he tossed scraps of bread to feed them. Jackdaws came whirling from the cliffs and a raven croaked hoarsely from its perch on a rocky peak.

The water was deep blue, like the sky, and purple shadows hovered over it, as the waves gently rocked the cormorants fishing there. The little boy leaned back in his sheltered spot, and the sound of the water made him drowsy. The sweet air lulled him and his head began to droop.

Then he saw a sight so beautiful he had to rub his eyes to get the sleep out of them. The wintry sun made a pathway on the water, flickering with points of light on the crests of the waves, and down this golden lane came a tiny ship that seemed no larger than a toy. She moved swiftly through the water, making for the cove, and Tom cried out with joy and clapped his hands as she approached.

The wind filled the blue satin sails, and the sunbeams caught the mast of gold. On deck was a company of sailors dressed in white, and they were making music of some kind, for shrill squeaks and whistles and pipings came through the air. Tom leaned forward to watch them, and as the ship came nearer he could see that the little sailors were playing flutes, tootling a hornpipe, then whistling a carol.

He stared very hard at their pointed faces, and little pink ears. They were not sailor-men at all, but a crew of white mice! There were four-and-twenty of them – yes, twenty-four white mice with gold rings round their snowy necks, and gold rings in their ears!

The little ship sailed into the cove, through the barriers of sharp rocks, and the white mice hurried backward and forward, hauling at the silken ropes, casting the gold anchor, crying with high voices as the ship came to port close to the rock where Tom sat waiting and watching.

Out came the Captain – and would you believe it? He was a Duck, with a cocked hat like Nelson's, and a blue jacket trimmed with gold braid. Tom knew at once he was Captain Duck because under his wing he carried a brass telescope, and by his side was a tiny sword.

He stepped boldly down the gangway and waddled to the eager little boy.

"Quack! Quack!" said the Captain, saluting Tom, and

132

Tom of course stood up and saluted back.

"The ship's cargo is ready, Sir," said the Duck. "We have sailed across the sea to wish you a merry Christmas. You will find everything in order, Sir. My men will bring the merchandise ashore, and here is the Bill of Lading."

The Duck held out a piece of seaweed, and Tom took it. "Thank you, Captain Duck," said he. "I'm not a very good reader yet, but I can count up to twenty-four."

"Quack! Quack!" cried the Duck, saluting again. "Quick! Quick!" he said, turning to the ship, and the four-and-twenty white mice scurried down to the cabin and dived into the hold.

Then up on deck they came, staggering under their burdens, dragging small bales of provisions, little oaken casks, baskets, sacks and hampers. They raced down the

ship's ladders, and clambered over the sides, and swarmed down the gangway. They brought their packages ashore and laid them on the smooth sand near Tom's feet.

There were almonds and raisins, bursting from silken sacks. There were sugar-plums and goodies, pouring out of wicker baskets. There was a host of tiny toys, drums and marbles, tops and balls, pearly shells, and a flying kite, a singing bird and a musical-box.

When the last toy had been safely carried from the ship the white mice scampered back. They weighed anchor, singing "Yo-heave-ho!" and they ran up the rigging. The Captain cried "Quack! Quack!" and he stood on the ship's bridge. Before Tom could say "Thank you", the little golden ship began to sail away, with flags flying, and the blue satin sails tugging at the silken cords. The four-and-twenty white mice waved their sailor hats to Tom, and the Captain looked at him through his spy-glass.

Away went the ship, swift as the wind, a glittering speck on the waves. Away she went towards the far horizon along that bright path that the sun makes when it shines on water.

Tom waited till he could see her no more, and then he stooped over his presents. He tasted the almonds and raisins, he sucked the goodies, he beat the drum, and tinkled the musical-box and the iron triangle. He flew the kite, and tossed the balls in the air, and listened to the song of the singing-bird. He was so busy playing that he did not hear soft footsteps behind him.

Suddenly he was lifted up in a pair of strong arms and pressed against a thick blue coat, and two bright eyes were smiling at him.

"Well, Thomas, my son! Here I am! You didn't expect me, now did you? A Happy Christmas, Tom, boy. I crept down soft as a snail, and you never heard a twinkle of me, did you?"

"Oh, Father!" Tom flung his arms round his father's neck and kissed him many times. "Oh, Father. I knew you were coming. Look! They've been, they came just before you, in the ship."

"Who, Tom? Who's been? I caught you fast asleep. Come along home and see what Father Christmas has brought you. He came along o' me, in my ship, you know. He gave me some presents for you."

"He's been here already, just now, in a little gold ship, Father," cried Tom, stammering with excitement. "He's just sailed away. He was a Duck, Captain Duck, and there were four-and-twenty white mice with him. He left me all these toys. Lots of toys and things."

Tom struggled to the ground, and pointed to the sand,

but where the treasure of the fairy ship had been stored there was only a heap of pretty shells and seaweed and striped pebbles.

"They're all gone," he cried, choking back a sob, but his father laughed and carried him off, pick-a-back, up the narrow footpath to the cottage.

"You've been dreaming, my son," said he. "Father Christmas came with me, and he's brought you a fine lot of toys, and I've got them at home for you."

"Didn't dream," insisted Tom. "I saw them all."

On the table in the kitchen lay such a medley of presents that Tom opened his eyes wider than ever. There were almonds and raisins in little coloured sacks, and a musical-box with a picture of a ship on its round lid. There was a drum with scarlet edges, and a book, and a pearly shell from a far island, and a kite of thin paper from China, and a love-bird in a cage. Best of all there was a little model of his father's ship, which his father had carved for Tom.

"Why, these are like the toys from the fairy ship," cried Tom. "Those were very little ones, like fairy toys, and these are big ones, real ones."

"Then it must have been a dream-ship," said his mother. "You must tell us all about it."

So little Tom told the tale of the ship with blue satin sails and gold mast, and he told of the four-and-twenty white mice with gold rings round their necks, and the Captain Duck, who said "Quack! Quack!" His father sat listening, as the words came tumbling from the excited little boy.

When Tom had finished, the sailor said, "I'll sing you a song of that fairy-ship, our Tom. Then you'll never forget what you saw."

He waited a moment, gazing into the great fire on the

hearth, and then he stood up and sang this song to his son
and to his wife.

> There was a ship a-sailing,
> A-sailing on the sea.
> And it was deeply laden,
> With pretty things for me.
>
> There were raisins in the cabin,
> And almonds in the hold,
> The sails were made of satin,
> And the mast it was of gold.
>
> The four-and-twenty sailors
> That stood between the decks
> Were four-and-twenty white mice
> With rings about their necks.

The Captain was a Duck, a Duck,
With a jacket on his back,
And when this fairy-ship set sail,
The Captain he said "Quack".

"Oh, sing it again," cried Tom, clapping his hands, and his father sang once more the song that later became a nursery rhyme.

It was such a lovely song that Tom hummed it all that happy Christmas Day, and it just fitted into the tune on his musical-box. He sang it to his children when they were little, long years later, and you can sing it too if you like!

TOBY, THE BEANS
AND THE HEDGEHOG

Nancy Blishen

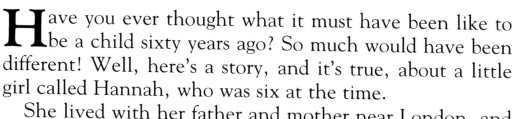

Have you ever thought what it must have been like to be a child sixty years ago? So much would have been different! Well, here's a story, and it's true, about a little girl called Hannah, who was six at the time.

She lived with her father and mother near London, and her best friend was her dog Toby. Toby's father had been an Alsatian, and his mother a Corgi. So Toby was a rather funny shape. He had a long body, rather like a sausage, very short legs, a head like an Alsatian's with long pointed ears, and a great feathery tail. When Hannah took him for a walk in long grass, all you could see of Toby was his ears and the tip of that feathery tail.

Hannah's Granny and Grandpa lived in the country and sometimes she went to stay there, always taking Toby with her. Hannah loved Granny's house. It smelt of apples; and instead of electric light, there were oil lamps. But what she liked best of all was going to bed. You may think this strange. Most boys and girls of six I know will try anything to put off going to bed. But there was something special about going to bed in Granny's house. If it was winter Granny would say, "Time to get down the warming pan!" Then Hannah would carefully lift down, from its hook by

the fire, something that was made of copper, had a long wooden handle, and looked like a very flat saucepan. Granny would go to the fire and, with the tongs, take out several hot coals. She'd put these in the pan, close the lid and, with a flickering candle in her hand, take Hannah upstairs. Then she'd rub the warming pan over the big, fluffy bed, and Hannah would jump into that warm nest. She'd sink down into the feathers until nothing could be seen of her but the tip of her nose.

But the story I want to tell you is about something that happened in summer time. Round Granny's house, wrapped all the way round it, was a beautiful big garden. Grandpa was enormously proud of his flowers and vegetables. He was especially proud of his runner beans. They climbed up poles – rows and rows and rows of them, all very straight and neat.

One day Hannah was filling her pocket with nuts from a tree at the end of the garden when she noticed that some of the bean plants were behaving oddly. They were wobbling and jumping about. Some were even leaning sideways! She hurried to the spot and – oh, dear! There was Toby, feathery tail and all, digging an enormous hole right in the middle of Grandpa's rows of beans. And right in the middle of that enormous hole was a little hedgehog, curled up tight, a prickly ball.

Now, Hannah knew that Granny and Grandpa were asleep in their armchairs. They were having what Granny called forty winks, though it sometimes went on so long that Hannah thought they might have been fifty or sixty winks, or even seventy. Anyway, there was time, surely, before they woke, to do something about Toby and the beans and the hedgehog. So she rushed off and got her little garden spade and gently lifted the hedgehog out of the hole. He scuttled off into the bushes, looking very put out, while Hannah held on to Toby's collar so he could not follow.

"Oh, Toby, how could you?" cried Hannah. And Toby dropped his ears and his tail and looked very sorry for himself. He'd been having a good time. What was wrong with that?

Hannah filled in the hole as best she could and straightened up the beans; and then she took Toby back to the house just as the kettle on the fire began to boil, ready for tea. Grandpa said:

"I think I'll go and water my beans before it gets dark. I'll be back in no time for a cup of tea and a slice of that cherry cake I saw you taking out of the oven this morning."

Well, poor Hannah! She loved Grandpa very much. But sometimes his eyes were fierce under his bushy white eyebrows. She wondered if he'd guess it was Toby who had disturbed his beans. She heard his footsteps going through the kitchen, and the back door opening and shutting. She waited, trembling. And after what seemed ages she heard the back door open again, and shut, and Grandpa's voice. "That wretched cat from next door! He's been scratching about among my beans!" And she heard Granny say, "Oh dear! Oh dear!"

And Hannah breathed an enormous sigh of relief and took a very large bite of cherry cake. As for Toby, he looked out from under the table where he'd been hiding and closed one eye. It looked for all the world as though he were winking.

And if you're wondering how I know about this – well, I was Hannah!

THE CAT AND THE PARROT

Virginia Haviland

Once upon a time a cat and a parrot agreed to ask each other to dinner in turn. First the cat would ask the parrot, then the parrot would invite the cat, and so on.

The cat in his turn was so stingy that he provided nothing for dinner but a pint of milk, a small slice of fish, and a bit of rice —which the parrot had to cook himself! He was too polite to complain, but he did not find it a good meal.

When it was the parrot's turn to entertain the cat, he cooked a great dinner, and did it before his guest arrived. Most tempting of all he offered was a clothes-basketful of crisp, brown cakes. He put four hundred and ninety-eight spicy cakes before the cat, and kept only two for himself.

Well, the cat ate every bit of the good food prepared by the parrot and began on the pile of cakes. He ate the four hundred and ninety-eight, then asked for more.

"Here are my two cakes," said the parrot. "You may eat them."

143

The cat ate the two cakes. He then looked around and asked for still more.

"Well," said the parrot, "I don't see anything more, unless you wish to eat me!"

The cat showed no shame. Slip! Slop! Down his throat went the parrot!

An old woman who happened to be near saw all this and threw a stone at the cat. "How dreadful to eat your friend the parrot!"

"Parrot, indeed!" said the cat. "What's a parrot? I've a great mind to eat you, too." And before you could say a word, slip! slop! down went the old woman!

The cat started down the road, feeling fine. Soon he met a man driving a donkey. When the man saw the cat he said, "Run away, cat, or my donkey might kick you to death."

"Donkey, indeed!" said the cat. "I have eaten five hundred cakes, I've eaten my friend the parrot, I've eaten an old woman. What's to keep me from eating an old man

and a donkey?" Slip! Slop! Down went the old man and the donkey.

The cat next met the wedding procession of a king. Behind the king and his new bride marched a column of soldiers and behind them a row of elephants, two by two. The king said to the cat, "Run away, cat, or my elephants might trample you to death."

"Ho!" said the cat. "I've eaten five hundred cakes, I've eaten my friend the parrot, I've eaten an old woman, I've eaten an old man and a donkey. What's to keep me from eating a beggarly king?"

Slip! Slop! Down went the king, the queen, the soldiers, and all the elephants!

The cat went on until he met two land crabs, scuttling along in the dusk. "Run away, cat," they squeaked, "or we will nip you!"

"Ho! Ho! Ho!" laughed the cat, shaking his fat sides. "I've eaten five hundred cakes, I've eaten my friend the parrot, I've eaten an old woman, I've eaten an old man with a donkey, I've eaten a king and a queen, his soldiers, and all his elephants. Shall I run away from land crabs? No. I'll eat you, too!"

Slip! Slop! Down went the land crabs.

When the land crabs got down inside the cat, they found themselves among a crowd of creatures. They could see the unhappy king with his bride, who had fainted. The soldiers were trying to march, and the elephants trumpeted while the donkey brayed as the old man beat it. The old woman and the parrot were there, and last of all, the five hundred cakes neatly piled in a corner.

The land crabs ran around to see what they could do. "Let's nip!" they said. So, nip! nip! nip! they made a round hole in the side of the cat. Nip! nip! nip! until the hole was big enough to let them all walk through. The land crabs scuttled out and away. Then out walked the king, carrying his bride; out walked the soldiers and the elephants, two by two; out walked the old man, driving his donkey; out walked the old woman, giving the cat a piece of her mind; and last of all, out walked the parrot with a cake in each claw!

HOW THE LITTLE BOY AND THE LITTLE GIRL WENT FOR A WALK IN THE MUD

A French fairy tale

Once upon a time there were a little boy and a little girl, and one day they decided to go for a walk. As it had just been pouring with rain, there was mud everywhere. And as there was mud everywhere, the path where the little boy and the little girl were walking was muddy too. And because the path was so very muddy, the little girl's feet suddenly slid from under her and – oops! – she fell smack into the mud on her little bottom.

The little boy then felt sorry for the little girl, so he caught hold of her with both his hands and began to pull her to her feet. As he was pulling her, his feet suddenly slid from under him and – oops! – he fell smack into the mud on his little bottom.

Then the little girl felt sorry for the little boy, so she caught hold of him with both her hands and began to pull him to his feet. As she was pulling him, her feet suddenly slid from under her and – oops! – she fell smack into the mud on her little bottom.

And so it went on:
oops! he sat smack in the mud,
oops! she sat smack in the mud,
oops! his bottom in,
oops! her bottom in,
oops! he fell,
oops! she fell,
oops! his turn,
oops! her turn,
and oops!
and oops!
And if they are still alive, they must still be in that mud, going oops!
and oops!
and oops!
and oops!

KING MIDAS
A Greek legend

This story begins on a hot day, in the fields surrounding a royal palace in Greece, long ago. The sun was as golden as it's ever been, and everything seemed gold in the shine of it. The stones of the palace were really white, but they seemed bright gold. The wheat in the fields was more gold than green, and the small prince lying asleep in the wheat seemed himself to be made of gold.

As for his nurse, who came looking for him – she too, her dress and her hair, shone as she walked. And the wheat rustled as she came through it as if it really had been of stiff bright gold. When she caught sight of the boy, she hurried forward and stood staring down at him, for a long time. Then she gently brushed his face, picked him up and hurried with him to the palace. She had a story to tell that the king, his father, must hear.

"Your Majesty," she said, "they were ants! First one, then another, they crawled out of the wheat and on to Prince Midas's shoulder, and so on to his face . . ."

"Well, my good woman," said the king. "If my little son *will* fall asleep in the wheat, he must expect that ants will climb over him. What do you wish me to do? Shall I order them to be executed for daring to walk on a royal face?"

"Your Majesty," cried the nurse. "Each ant carried a grain of wheat."

"Indeed!" said the king. "But ants were always thieves. Do you want me to call for my soldiers and make war on the ants for stealing my wheat?"

"But, Your Majesty," said the nurse, "as each ant came to Prince Midas's mouth, it laid its grain of wheat there and returned the way it had come. Each ant did this in turn – laid its grains of wheat on the prince's mouth and then went away. It was strange! Strange! It was as if they knew what they were doing, and meant something by it!"

"That is different," said the king. "Our ants are thieves, but they carry messages from the gods as well as any other living creature. This was a sign from the gods. My wise men will know what it means."

And indeed the wise men did know. It meant, they said, that one day Prince Midas would be wonderfully rich. It was certainly a sign from the gods. As plain as if they had spoken, the ants were saying, in taking the grains of wheat to the prince's mouth and leaving them there, that some day he would be *fabulously* rich.

And so the prince grew up with that story in his ears, the story of the sign the gods had given. His nurse talked about it often.

"Ah, my young lord," she would say, "one day the palace will be yours, and the fields about it, and the whole kingdom."

"But that won't be all, will it?" the prince would cry. "Tell me again, nurse – what *more* shall I have?"

"Oh my lord," the nurse would say, "how can I tell? I am only your poor nurse and never have more than a few common coins in my pocket. So how can I tell you of all the gold you shall have one day – more gold than any king has ever had who ever ruled the earth!"

"Shall I have the sun, too, nurse?" the prince would ask. "For that is the goldest thing of all!"

"My lord," the nurse would say, "how can I tell? Perhaps you will have the sun, though surely the sun belongs to the gods. I think you will have all the gold the gods can spare."

The years passed and the prince became king in his father's place. He married a king's daughter and had a daughter of his own: and though he loved his wife, and his child, and enjoyed being king, still he was not content. When would the time come that the gods had promised, when he would be fabulously rich?

And then one day an old man came to the palace. He was not like ordinary men. He was taller, and older, than men ever are: his eyes shone as the eyes of men never shine. He'd been found wandering and lost near the palace. King Midas knew at once that this old man came from the world of the gods. His name was Silenus, he told the king. He was the close friend of the god Bacchus. Bacchus was the god of merry-making. And merry they'd been, the god and his old friend! So merry that Silenus had fallen asleep from all the laughing and dancing and drinking of wine. And when he woke up, he was alone and lost, there in Midas's kingdom.

So Midas gave him food, and wine, and a bed to sleep in. And for twelve days there was laughing and dancing and drinking of wine, in honour of this visitor from the world of the gods. And on the thirteenth day Midas himself went with Silenus to the mountain where the gods lived. It was called Olympus: and there they found the god Bacchus, who was overjoyed by the return of his friend.

"King Midas," said the god, "you have done me great

service. I had thought my old friend was lost for ever. What reward will you have? I will give you whatever you wish."

And Midas thought of that old promise. "If you would give me what I wish," he cried, "what I wish for with all my heart, then . . . oh, let everything I touch turn to gold!"

Bacchus had been smiling, but now his smile vanished. "Midas," he said. "I must give it to you if it is really what you wish, for I have promised. But the gods can see further than men can see. That is a bad wish! Wish for anything but that!"

"But how can there be a better wish?" asked Midas. "Since I was a child lying under the sun I have loved whatever is gold. I have no other wish than this. Let this be my reward."

The god sighed. "It shall be so, then," he said. "But I grant your wish with a heavy heart, King Midas. Now go and . . . enjoy it as best you can."

Enjoy it! Oh, thought Midas, as he made his way down from the mountain, how could he fail to enjoy this great gift? Now he would be the richest man on earth! He was so excited that he kept putting off the moment when he would touch something with his magic touch. Not until he had set foot in his own kingdom again, and was passing through a grove of olive trees, did he reach out a hand. It was a trembling, excited hand. And with it, he touched a hanging leaf. Strange! *Strange!* There was the leaf, soft in his hand as leaves are, and then it was heavy, it was stiff, it glittered – it was pure gold!

"Oh," cried Midas. "I can make gold with my touch! A golden leaf! A whole golden tree! Tree after tree of pure gold! Listen to the golden leaves tinkling in the breeze!" He was running wildly towards the palace, touching trees, and stones, and flowers as he went, and leaving them glittering behind him. "I can turn the very dirt into gold!" he cried. "I can turn the earth I walk on into gold!"

Now he had reached the palace. He touched its wall, as he came to it, and the rough warm stones turned smooth and bright and cold. He thought of all the things he would touch – all the common things he would turn into precious brightness and glitter. On the low branch of a tree sat a bird, a small bird, one of the palace birds so tame that it would take food from the hands of the king or the queen or their daughter. Now Midas held out his hand towards it. And the bird flew to his hand, as it always did. Warm, soft feathers, beating heart, beak open ready to sing, wings stirring. And in a second, in less than a second, it was a hard, cold, magnificent bird of solid gold! And Midas put it in his pocket and hurried into the palace.

At once he cried for food and drink. "I've been far, and

come far, and I have wonderful news!" he told the queen. "But first let me eat and drink. I shall tell you nothing of my news until I have eaten."

In no time a meal was ready, and the king and his queen and his daughter and all the court sat down. Everyone was longing to hear this marvellous news that Midas spoke of. Everyone was wondering why the king was so excited, so happy. The long journey had made Midas hungrier than ever before, and he reached eagerly for the food in front of him. It was good – good warm food with a good warm smell to it! He lifted it to his lips, and the warmth went, the smell went. His lips touched something hard, and cold.

The food in his hand had turned to gold.

Suddenly he was terrified. He dropped the golden food, and reached for the glass of wine at his side. It was cool and sweet – cool, sweet wine with a cool, sweet smell. He lifted it to his lips – and they touched something hard, and cold. The glass in his hand, and the wine in the glass, had turned to gold.

The queen, and their young daughter, and all the court were staring at the king. They didn't understand what was happening.

"Don't be afraid," cried Midas. "My friends, don't be afraid! You see, this is my wonderful news. The god Bacchus has granted my dearest wish, and everything I touch turns to gold. I shall be the richest of all the men that ever lived. My daughter! I have a gift for you in my pocket – look, a bird that I touched and that straightway turned to gold. Here it is, my dear daughter!"

And he held out the golden bird. Even as he did so, he saw the danger, and cried, *"Ah, don't touch my hand!"*

But it was too late. The little girl had reached out for the

154

glittering bird, and as her hand touched his, she froze into solid gold. Her warm flesh, her soft hair, turned to stiff, shining gold. Her dark eyes became fixed and golden. All the life left her, and she leaned gold and silent across the table with her gold hand on her father's hand.

And now there was terror in the palace.

People shrank away from the king. They dreaded that he might touch them. As for Midas, his heart had turned heavy within him when his beloved daughter changed into that dead glittering gold child. But still he could not believe that his power was a bad power. How could it be? Gold was the most precious thing in the world, surely. He could make gold with his touch. He went through the palace – the terrified, silent palace – and he touched the chairs and the tables. He touched his throne and the queen's throne, and everything turned to gold. Everywhere was the cold flash and gleam of gold! He turned glass to gold, and now you could not see through the glass. He turned cloth to gold, and now the cloth no longer stirred as it hung. He turned the palace dogs to gold, and now they no longer yawned and stretched themselves or leapt to greet the king when he came near them.

Already he had so much gold that he was twice as rich – three times as rich – now, ten times as rich – as any other king on earth. He called for the queen to come and share his joy.

"My love! My love!" he called. "Come and see how I can turn things to gold!"

But the queen had hidden herself. She was weeping for her golden daughter. She was weeping for Midas. Never again would she dare to be near the king. How could she, when one touch would turn her into a dead gold queen!

155

And now Midas's joy began to turn into terror. How was he to eat or drink, when what he tried to eat or drink turned at once into glittering metal? He longed to touch someone's hand, to stroke a dog and feel the living fur under his fingers. He longed to feel one thing warm, another soft, one thing rough and another smooth. He longed for the sight of wood, cloth, flesh. He longed for the poorest and commonest things in the world. He longed for stones, and for the earth itself. But everywhere he went there was the gold he had made. Everything in his silent palace was silent, gleaming gold. The very clothes he touched turned to gold. How could you wear clothes of stiff, chilly gold? In his hunger and his anger he beat his fist against a wall and the wall turned to gold.

"What shall I do? What shall I do?" he cried. "I'm the richest man in the world, but I'm the hungriest and the loneliest! This cursed gift the god gave me!" Then he wondered if Bacchus would take the gift back again. But *no*, he thought – *no*, he would not give it up! It was such a marvellous gift! Whatever happened, he would keep it!

And he sat on his golden throne, in his golden throne room, and tried to believe he was happy. He *must* be happy, because he was so rich!

And it was there his old nurse found him. She was not his nurse now, of course – instead, she looked after his daughter. She was a brave woman, for she was the only person in Midas's kingdom who dared come near him.

"Oh, there you are, my lord," she cried. "This won't do, you know! How could you be so silly?"

"Nurse, watch your tongue!" Midas growled.

"You should have watched your tongue yourself, my lord," said the nurse, "before you asked for this foolish gift.

156

Now there's only one thing to do: you must go to the god and ask him to take his gift back."

"I won't," said Midas, sulkily. It was as if he was a young prince again, and she was still his nurse.

"Now, just think for a minute," she said. "How would you like a fine meal – good meat, savoury things and sweet things? Fruit! And wine to drink!"

"Stop!" cried Midas. "Nurse, stop!"

"How would you like to wear soft, warm cloth again, instead of those stupid cold clothes of gold?"

"Nurse!" he cried. "Stop! I command you to say no more!"

"And how would you like to take your daughter in your arms again? How would you like to hug her? How would you like to hold the hand of the queen?"

"Nurse! Nurse!" cried the king. "No more! I will go! I will go back to the god!"

And that's what he did. He went alone, across his kingdom, to the home of the gods on the mountain, Olympus. And there he begged Bacchus to take back the gift he had given him.

"I expected you to come," said the god. "The gods do not always take back the gifts they have given. But your suffering has been great. I will remove this power from you. Listen carefully. Go from here to the great river that runs through your kingdom. Lie in the river and let the water run over you. Then it will be the river that has the power to make gold, and you will be an ordinary man again."

And so Midas hurried back down the mountain to his kingdom. He ran through the olive grove where he had first turned things into gold. He ran past the golden trees, stiff and shining, down to the river. And he stretched himself out in the river, until the water had washed over him again and again.

Now had he lost his awful power? To climb out of the river he must catch hold of a low branch growing on the bank. What if the branch turned to gold in his grasp? He took a deep breath, and seized it. There was the good feel of wood in his hand. It didn't turn cold and stiff, as he'd been used to things turning when he touched them. He pulled himself out of the water, and looked down at the river.

The little stones and the sand at the bottom glittered as if a thousand little suns were shining in the water. The power to turn what it touched to gold had passed to the river, and at the bottom of it for ever gold would be found, gold stones and gold sand.

And Midas ran back to his palace, to find that all the things he had turned to gold had become themselves again. There, waiting for him on the palace steps, was his daughter. On her warm, living hand the golden bird was perched – but now it was a warm, living bird.

"Father," called his daughter. "Oh father, look! The little bird wants to eat crumbs from your hand, as it always used to do! Here, father – hold it!"

Midas took the bird and felt its warm claws on his hand. The bird pecked at the crumbs in his hand, and he stroked the bird's head.

And from the bottom of his heart he thanked the god for taking back his foolish wish.

BRER RABBIT, HE'S A GOOD FISHERMAN

Joel Chandler Harris

One day, when Brer Rabbit, and Brer Fox, and Brer Bear and a whole lot of them was clearing a new ground for to plant a roasting-pear patch, the sun began to get sort of hot, and Brer Rabbit, he got tired; but he didn't let on, 'cause he feared the others would call him lazy, and he keep on carrying away rubbish and piling it up, till by and by he holler out that he got a thorn in his hand, and then he take and slip off, and hunt for a cool place for to rest. After a while he come across a well with a bucket hanging in it.

"That looks cool," says Brer Rabbit, says he. "And cool I 'specs she is. I'll just about get in there and take a nap," and with that, in he jump, he did, and he ain't no sooner fix himself than the bucket begin to go down. Brer Rabbit, he was mighty scared. He know where he come from, but he don't know where he's going. Suddenly he feel the bucket hit the water, and there she sat, but Brer Rabbit, he keep mighty still, 'cause he don't know what minute's going to be the next. He just lay there and shook and shiver.

Brer Fox always got one eye on Brer Rabbit, and when he slip off from the new ground, Brer Fox, he sneak after him. He knew Brer Rabbit was after some project or another, and he took and crope off, he did, and watch him. Brer Fox

see Brer Rabbit come to the top of the well and stop, and then he see him jump in the bucket, and then, lo and behold! he see him go down out of sight. Brer Fox was the most 'stonished fox that you ever laid eyes on. He sat down in the bushes and thought and thought, but he don't make no head nor tails of this kind of business. Then he say to himself, says he,

"Well, if this don't beat everything!" says he. "Right down there in that well Brer Rabbit keep his money hid, and if it ain't that, he done gone and 'scovered a gold mine, and if it ain't that, then I'm a-going to see what's in there."

Brer Fox crope up a little nearer, he did, and listen, but he don't hear no fuss, and he keep on getting nearer, and yet he don't hear nothing. By and by he get up close and peep down, but he don't see nothing, and he don't hear nothing. All this time Brer Rabbit was mighty near scared out of his skin, and he feared for to move 'cause the bucket might keel over and spill him in the water. While he was saying his prayers over and over, Brer Fox holler out,

"Heyo, Brer Rabbit! Who you visitin' down there?" says he.

"Who? Me? Oh, I'm just a-fishing, Brer Fox," says Brer Rabbit, says he. "I just say to myself that I'd sort of s'prise you all with a mess of fishes, and so here I is, and there's the fishes. I'm a-fishing for supper, Brer Fox," says Brer Rabbit, says he.

"Is there many of them down there, Brer Rabbit?" says Brer Fox, says he.

"Lots of them, Brer Fox, scores and scores of them. The water is naturally alive with them. Come down and help me haul them in, Brer Fox," says Brer Rabbit, says he.

"How I going to get down, Brer Rabbit?"

"Jump in the other bucket, Brer Fox. I'll fetch you down all safe and sound."

Brer Rabbit talked so happy and so sweet that Brer Fox he jump in the bucket, he did, and so he went down, 'cause his weight pulled Brer Rabbit up. When they pass one another on the half-way ground, Brer Rabbit he sing out:

> "Good-bye, Brer Fox, take care o' your clothes,
> For this is the way the world goes;
> Some goes up and some goes down,
> You'll get to the bottom all safe and soun'."

When Brer Rabbit got out, he gallop off and told the folks what the well belonged to, that Brer Fox was down there muddying up the drinking water, and then he gallop back to the well, and holler down to Brer Fox:

> "Here come a man with a great big gun –
> When he haul you up, you jump and run."

Well, soon enough Brer Fox was out of the well, and in just about half an hour both of them was back on the new ground working just as if they'd never heard of no well. But every now and then Brer Rabbit would burst out laughing, and old Brer Fox would scowl and say nothing.

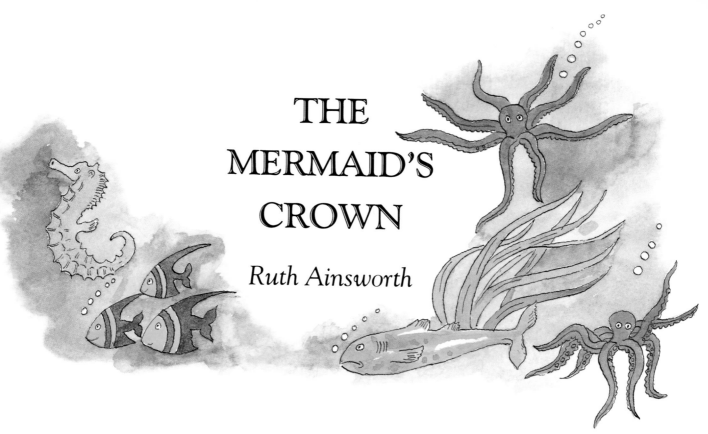

THE MERMAID'S CROWN

Ruth Ainsworth

Peter and Rose lived in a cottage by the sea. It had a tiny garden, but that did not matter. There were no parks or playgrounds nearby, but that was not important either. The children always played on the beach, summer and winter.

In the summer they scrambled over the rocks and paddled in the pools, and Rose made houses of stones and sand, with gardens of seaweed and shells. They were pretty enough to live in.

In the winter they often played in wellingtons and sometimes had to shelter in a cave or against a rock. But the beach was lovely to play on, all the year round.

They liked to play on a flat rock, jutting out into the sea with a pool on one side.

One winter's day, Rose was fishing bits of seaweed out of the pool to make a garden. The seaweed was cold and slippery and her hands were frozen, but she had nearly enough when, reaching out for a wavy purple ribbon, she

saw something floating deep down.

"Peter, come and help. I can see something lovely but I can't reach it. Hold my legs."

Peter held her legs tightly and she rolled up her sleeve and reached into the icy water.

"I've got it – no, it has slipped away – now I've got it again. Hold tight!"

She brought up something neither child had ever seen before. It was a circle of seaweed, not floppy, but firm, and mixed with the weed were shells and shining stones.

"It's like a crown," said Peter.

"And it's mine," said Rose, putting it on her head. "It's my very own." It fitted perfectly.

Their parents examined it and talked about it, but could not decide how it had got into the pool. Perhaps from a wreck? They thought the pink stones were coral and the yellow ones amber. After a few days of talking and wondering they lost interest.

Rose had only one safe place in the house, a wooden box with a lock which she called her treasure box. She kept the crown in this when she wasn't wearing it.

Christmas was getting near and their father put the tree in its tub in the sitting-room. That afternoon the children began to decorate it. All the decorations from previous years were kept in a big cardboard box. While they were busy, Rose suddenly cried out:

"Peter! Someone looked in at the window."

Peter turned round, but there was no one there. Then Rose called out again, "Look! Quickly!" This time Peter saw a face for an instant. Then it disappeared. He opened the window and jumped out and a little later appeared at the door, leading someone by the hand. It was a mermaid, or rather a mermaid child, about the size of Rose.

The mermaid had long, golden hair, sad grey eyes, a pale face and a fishy tail. At first she looked round the room in silence. Then she turned to Rose and spoke.

"I want my crown back."

"So it was yours," said Rose. "I didn't know whose it was. I found it floating in the pool. No one was bothering about it. It's mine now."

"But I want it."

"So do I," said Rose. "Will you have something off the Christmas tree instead? Something pretty?"

The mermaid liked the tree. She touched the baubles and the candles very gently and stroked the glass bird. She looked up at the angel who stood at the very top. Then she pointed to a string of tinsel, shining among the dark pine needles.

"Please. For my head."

Rose untwined the tinsel and put it round the mermaid's hair.

"Look in the glass," she said.

The mermaid balanced on a stool and looked at herself in the mirror on the wall.

"It will do," she said gravely and then, quick as a fish leaping, she flashed across the floor, out of the window, and away.

"I shan't tell mother about the mermaid," said Rose.

They almost forgot about the mermaid as the weeks went by and they saw no sign of her. Rose thought of her when she wore her crown and when she locked it in her treasure box. At Easter time they got their Easter eggs ready. The village shop only had plain chocolate ones but they wrapped them in coloured paper and tied them up with ribbon that their mother had given them. Suddenly they felt they were being watched. There, outside the window, was the mermaid. Peter let her in.

"I want my crown," she said. "The silver one came to pieces, bit by bit. There's nothing left."

"But I want it too," said Rose, "and it's mine now. Will

you choose a ribbon instead?"

The mermaid looked at the ribbons and touched a red one.

"For my hair, please."

Peter tied the bow as his bows were better than Rose's. Again the mermaid looked at herself in the mirror. Then, quick as a fish leaping, she slipped across the floor and out of the window and away.

Rose hoped she would never come back again, and once more she did not tell her mother what had happened. She did not often wear the crown either, though she looked at it almost every day. The seaweed still shone as if it were wet.

But it was not many weeks before the mermaid appeared a third time. The children were picking kingcups in the stream when she rose, suddenly, from the reeds nearby.

"I want my crown," she said. "The red one kept slipping off and the fishes nibbled it. It isn't pretty any more."

"You should never have let the old one go if you loved it so much," said Rose. "Shall I make you a wreath of kingcups? A golden crown?"

"A golden crown," repeated the mermaid. "Yes," and she almost smiled.

Rose made the crown like a daisy chain, slitting a stalk with her fingernail and drawing the next flower through. The mermaid looked at herself in the clear water.

"Gold," she whispered. "Better than silver or scarlet."

She flashed through the reeds and grasses and disappeared towards the seashore.

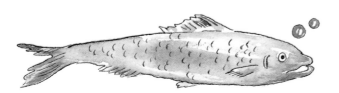

In less than a week she was back, her pale face pressed against the window.

"I must have my crown. The gold one drooped and faded and died. My father is a Lord of the Sea and he is going to a banquet with the other Lords. My mother and I are going too. We must all wear our crowns. So I need mine."

Rose saw two tears on the mermaid's cheeks and this time she did not hesitate.

"You shall have it. I'll fetch it."

She ran upstairs, unlocked her treasure box, and brought the crown down. The mermaid put it on and clapped her hands with joy.

"Come to the flat rock in three days' time," she said, before she flashed through the window. With a twist and a twirl, she was gone.

After three days the children went to the flat rock and

there, on a bed of seaweed, was an oyster shell. It was tightly closed. When their father opened it, there was a pearl inside. Rose kept it in her treasure box to be made into a ring for her, when she was older and her fingers had stopped growing.

"That will remind you of the mermaid for ever," said her mother, who now knew the whole story.

"I'll remember her even without a pearl," said Rose. "I'll remember her golden hair and her pale face and her fishy tail, and her lovely crown. I knew it was really hers, not mine."

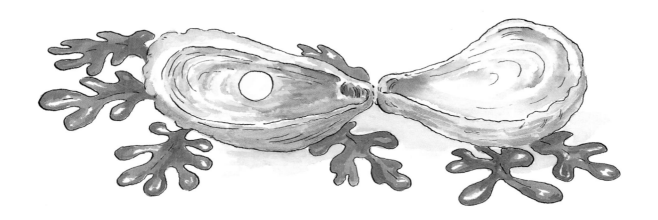

THE KING WHO WANTED TO WALK ON THE MOON

A Persian tale

There was once a king who wanted nothing so much as to walk on the moon. When he ought to have been ruling his country he was sitting about, thinking of the moon. There it was, up above his head. He could see it. Some nights, when it was bright and full, he felt he could touch it. But it was out of reach.

Being a king, he was used to doing anything he wished. But wish as much as he would, this was something he could *not* do. The king could not walk on the moon.

But one day he had an idea. Of course, of course! Build a tower! He would call together all the carpenters in his kingdom and order them to build a tower. Then he would climb it and step from the top straight on to the moon. That was it!

But the carpenters made long faces.

"Build a tower to the sky?" they cried.

"Yes," said the king, "to the sky."

"The *sky?*" And they pointed upwards. There was the sky, as far away as anything you could think of. "You can't mean the sky," they said.

"I *do* mean the sky," said the king. And he said if all the carpenters in his kingdom didn't start work at once, he'd call for all the executioners in his kingdom. There wouldn't be a carpenter left anywhere with a head on his shoulders.

So the carpenters, who didn't like the idea of having no heads on their shoulders, went off to buy wood. They bought huge quantities of wood, and they made measurements, and they bit their lips, and I'm afraid some of them bit their fingernails. But they couldn't see how you could make a wooden tower reaching to the sky. The king became very cross. He wanted to walk on the moon by next Saturday, at the latest. So he called the carpenters together *and* he called for his executioners, too.

"This is your last chance," he told the carpenters. "Start work tomorrow, or your heads will roll!"

So the carpenters, who didn't like the idea of their heads rolling, went away to think again. And they thought, and they thought, and they came up with an idea. They went back to the king and said they knew how to do it. But when it was finished it might be a rather dangerous tower to climb, so perhaps they should climb it first.

"Never!" cried the king. "Never! I'm not having a lot of carpenters reaching the moon before the king does. *I'll* do the climbing. You get on with the building. How do you mean to do it?"

And the carpenters told him of their plan. And he sent out all the heralds in his kingdom with a message to all the men, women and children in his kingdom that they were to bring to the palace every box they had, and all the boxes would be heaped on top of one another in the palace gardens. And at last the tower of boxes was bound to reach the sky.

Well, it didn't. It was wonderfully high, and wonderfully shaky, but it didn't reach the sky. So the king ordered all the trees in his kingdom to be chopped down by all the wood-cutters in his kingdom; and then all the box-makers in his kingdom

172

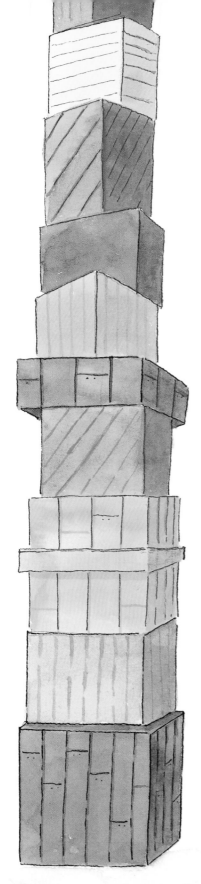

were ordered to turn the wood into boxes. When these boxes were added to the tower – well, you couldn't see the top of it. It was hidden in the clouds.

So the king started his climb. Up he went, up and up, and to the people on the ground he grew smaller and smaller. For a long time they could see his gold crown twinkling, but then they could no longer see that. For a long time they could see his silver shoes flashing, but then they could no longer see those. The clouds swallowed him up.

Then at last, out of the clouds, came a very small, very distant voice. They cupped their ears with their hands and one or two of them, who had especially good hearing, could just make out the king's words.

"I'm nearly there," he was crying. "I just want *one more box!*"

But there wasn't a box left in the kingdom. There wasn't a tree left. There wasn't a splinter of wood, anywhere. And when they shouted this news up to the king, all the people in his kingdom shouting at once so he could hear the message travelling miles up through the air, he became *very* angry. And they heard his voice again.

"All right," he said. "*All right!*" What they must do, then, was to pull a box out

from the bottom of the pile and send it up to him. That way he'd reach the moon.

Well, you can see what was wrong with that idea. Even the babies in his kingdom could see what was wrong with that. But if you'd rather have your head on than off, you don't disobey a king. So they did as they were ordered.

They pulled a box out from the bottom of the pile.

And the tower collapsed. The king came spinning out of the clouds. He came down much faster than he went up. And his crown dropped off as he fell and came twinkling through the air ahead of him.

I'll tell you one thing. It cured the king of wanting to walk on the moon.

WHY NOAH CHOSE THE DOVE

Isaac Bashevis Singer

When the people sinned and God decided to punish them by sending the flood, all the animals gathered around Noah's ark. Noah was a righteous man, and God had told him how to save himself and his family by building an ark that would float and shelter them when the waters rose.

The animals had heard a rumour that Noah was to take with him on the ark only the best of all the living creatures. So the animals came and vied with one another, each boasting about its own virtues and whenever possible belittling the merits of others.

The lion roared: "I am the strongest of all the beasts, and I surely must be saved."

The elephant blared: "I am the largest. I have the longest trunk, the biggest ears, and the heaviest feet."

"To be big and heavy is not so important," yapped the fox. "I, the fox, am the cleverest of all."

"What about me?" brayed the donkey. "I thought I was the cleverest."

"It seems anyone can be clever," yipped the skunk. "I

smell the best of all the animals. My perfume is famous."

"All of you scramble over the earth, but I'm the only one that can climb trees," shrieked the monkey.

"Only one!" growled the bear. "What do you think I do?"

"And how about me?" chattered the squirrel indignantly.

"I belong to the tiger family," purred the cat.

"I'm a cousin of the elephant," squeaked the mouse.

"I'm just as strong as the lion," snarled the tiger. "And I have the most beautiful fur."

"My spots are more admired than your stripes," the leopard spat back.

"I am man's closest friend," yelped the dog.

"You're no friend. You're just a fawning flatterer," bayed the wolf. "I am proud. I'm a lone wolf and flatter no one."

"Baa!" blatted the sheep. "That's why you're always hungry. Give nothing, get nothing. I give man my wool, and he takes care of me."

"You give man wool, but I give him sweet honey," droned the bee. "Besides, I have venom to protect me from my enemies."

"What is your venom compared with mine?" rattled the snake. "And I am closer to Mother Earth than any of you."

"Not as close as I am," protested the earthworm, sticking its head out of the ground.

"I lay eggs," clucked the hen.

"I give milk," mooed the cow.

"I help man plough the earth," bellowed the ox.

"I carry man," neighed the horse. "And I have the largest eyes of all of you."

"You have the largest eyes, but you have only two, while I have many," the housefly buzzed right into the horse's ear.

"Compared with me, you're all midgets." The giraffe's

words came from a distance as he nibbled the leaves off the top of a tree.

"I'm almost as tall as you are," chortled the camel. "And I can travel in the desert for days without food or water."

"You two are tall, but I'm fat," snorted the hippopotamus. "And I'm pretty sure that my mouth is bigger than anybody's."

"Don't be so sure," snapped the crocodile, and yawned.

"I can speak like a human," squawked the parrot.

"You don't really speak – you just imitate," the rooster crowed. "I know only one word, 'cock-a-doodle-doo', but it is my own."

"I see with my ears; I fly by hearing," piped the bat.

"I sing with my wing," chirped the cricket.

There were many more creatures who were eager to praise themselves. But Noah had noticed that the dove was perched alone on a branch and did not try to speak and compete with the other animals.

"Why are you silent?" Noah asked the dove. "Don't you have anything to boast about?"

"I don't think of myself as better or wiser or more attractive than the other animals," cooed the dove. "Each one of us has something the other doesn't have, given us by God who created us all."

"The dove is right," Noah said. "There is no need to boast and compete with one another. God has ordered me to take creatures of all kinds into the ark, cattle and beast, bird and insect."

The animals were overjoyed when they heard these words, and all their grudges were forgotten.

Before Noah opened the door of the ark, he said, "I love all of you, but because the dove remained modest and silent while the rest of you bragged and argued, I choose it to be my messenger."

Noah kept his word. When the rains stopped, he sent the dove to fly over the world and bring back news of how things were. At last she returned with an olive leaf in her beak, and Noah knew that the waters had receded. When the land finally became dry, Noah and his family and all the animals left the ark.

After the flood God promised that never again would he destroy the earth because of man's sins, and that seed time and harvest, cold and heat, summer and winter, day and night would never cease.

The truth is that there are in the world more doves than there are tigers, leopards, wolves, vultures, and other ferocious beasts. The dove lives happily without fighting. It is the bird of peace.

THE LITTLE POT AND THE FLOOD OF PORRIDGE

A tale from Germany

There was once a poor widow who had a little cottage, a *very* little garden, and a daughter. They ate what they could grow in the garden and when summer came, the daughter would go into the wood and pick wild strawberries.

She was doing that one bright day, and had had a good morning. Her basket was half-full already. It was time for lunch. So she sat on a fallen tree and prepared to eat the piece of bread she'd brought with her. She thought she might eat a few wild strawberries, too. There was a little brook nearby, with clear sweet water running in it. She'd drink from that when she was ready.

And at that moment, as it seemed out of nowhere, an old woman appeared. She was very small, and had a hunched back and a kindly face. She was holding a little pot.

"Oh, my darling," she said, in a little fluty sort of voice. "I'm *so* hungry! I have eaten nothing since the day before the day before the day before yesterday. Would you give me a bite of that bread in your hand?"

"It's rather hard bread – we can't afford anything better," said the girl. "But of course you can have some. Indeed, take it all. I shall soon be going home, and I can eat there. But mind your teeth. It *is* hard!"

"Bless you, my darling," said the old woman. "You're a good, kind girl. But I must give you something for it. Here, take this pot. It's a rather special pot. You've only got to say, 'Little pot, what about some porridge?' and at once it will cook porridge for you. And when the pot is full, you must say, 'Little pot, that's enough!' and it will stop. But you must remember the exact words. No other words will do. Alas, it wouldn't work for me. That is why I am so hungry. But for you, I know it will work."

And the old woman bit into the bread, hard though it was, handed over the little pot, and vanished as she had come.

When the girl arrived home she showed her mother first the basket full of wild strawberries, and then the mysterious little pot. Feeling very excited, they placed the pot on the table and the girl said, "Little pot, what about some porridge?" The pot had been absolutely empty, but now, from the bottom of it, porridge came bubbling. A little porridge, and then a little more, and then a lot of porridge, till the pot was full. Then the girl said, "Little pot, that's enough!" and at once the pot stopped producing porridge. And the widow and her daughter fetched their spoons and – my, that was *good* porridge! It was good, sweet porridge! Not for a long time had they felt so contented after a meal.

The next day (after they'd had guess-what for breakfast), the girl went off again to pick wild strawberries. She hadn't been gone long before the widow felt hungry again. So she put the pot on the table and said, "Little pot, what about some porridge?" And to her joy, it worked for her too. At once the little pot began filling with thick, wholesome, sweet porridge.

Now the old woman's porridge bowl, and her spoon,

were out in the kitchen, where they'd been washed up after breakfast. So the widow trotted out to get them, and when she returned – oh my! The porridge was pouring out of the pot. Actually, it had poured out of the pot on to the table, and off the table on to a chair, and off the chair on to the floor, and now it was pouring across the floor. The widow was so horrified she couldn't remember the words that would make the little pot stop.

"Oh, little pot, please don't!" she cried. "Please, you awkward little pot, *that will do!*" she cried again, and then, "Oh please, pot – please, *please*, PLEASE!"

But the pot paid no attention, for those were quite the wrong words. The widow tried to stop the porridge by covering the bowl with a cloth. But the porridge simply

pushed the cloth out of the way, and now in the room there was a kind of flood of porridge. It had covered the floor, and was rising up the walls, and if the widow had stayed she'd have suffered a very strange death. She'd have drowned in porridge, which not many people do. But she ran up the stairs to the bedroom and then, as the porridge began to climb the stairs, she pulled herself up into the loft.

By now the porridge had forced open the front door of the cottage, and the back door, and was pouring out into the little garden, and into the street. It broke the windows, too, and poured out of them. The street was soon a river of porridge, and the village green had become a great porridge pond. And some people who'd been out of doors when this happened had to climb trees, or they would have been up to

their waists in porridge. And still it came. The widow had climbed out of the topmost window and on to the roof. But still the level of the porridge rose.

And at that moment, thank goodness, the widow's daughter appeared. She had filled her basket with wild strawberries in record time. As soon as she saw what was happening, she called out, "Little pot, that's enough!"

And the pot stopped cooking porridge.

I'm afraid the widow had to stay on the roof of the cottage and the villagers had to stay up the trees until they got rid of all that porridge. Which they did only when all the other villagers got together and ate their way through it, until there was only a little porridge left. And they all had dreadful indigestion.

After which, they had to clean the place again. As someone said, it was the first time they'd ever had a whole village to wash up.

BRAINBOX

Philippa Pearce

Once upon a time a horse lived by himself in a large meadow. His name was Brainbox; but he was not really a clever horse at all. In his meadow Brainbox had grass to eat and a stream to drink from; but he had no company. He felt very lonely. He needed another horse to be his friend.

One day Brainbox could bear his loneliness no longer. He trotted to the far end of his meadow; then he turned and began to canter, then to gallop towards the other end. He galloped as fast as he could – faster and faster – until he reached the hedge, and then he JUMPED. He cleared the hedge, jumping right out of his meadow altogether and into the lane on the other side.

"This is a lane," said Brainbox to himself. "If I go along it, perhaps I shall find another horse to be my friend." He began to trot down the lane. As he went, he kept a sharp look-out for another horse.

One thing was worrying Brainbox: he was not certain of recognizing another horse if he saw one. He had lived alone in his meadow for so long that he could not remember what other horses looked like. "And if I can't remember that," said Brainbox to himself, "then I've nothing to go on, have I?" He was not a very clever horse.

He was not clever, but he was determined. "I shall just

have to ask," said Brainbox. "Ask and ask and ask again."

The first creature he saw in the lane was a snake – a harmless grass-snake. The snake was gliding among the grasses at the side of the lane.

Brainbox called: "Wait, you there!"

The snake paused a moment.

"Are you a horse?" asked Brainbox. "Because I'm looking for a horse to be my friend."

The snake gazed at him in amazement. "Sssssilly – sssso ssssilly!" hissed the snake. "Can't you see I'm not a horse? I'm a snake."

"How can one tell the difference?" asked Brainbox.

"Horses have legs, for one thing," said the snake. "Snakes haven't – they don't need them. Watch!" And, legless, the snake glided swiftly away and out of sight among the grasses.

"Well, now, that's a useful bit of information, for a start," said the not-so-very-clever Brainbox. "Now I know that I have to find a creature with legs, if I'm to find a horse to be my friend."

And he trotted on down the lane.

The next creature he saw in the lane was a hen who had strayed from her hen-run. She was pecking about in the lane when the horse caught sight of her. She pecked here at a seed, there at an insect, and as she pecked she ran to and fro. "On legs!" said Brainbox to himself. So he called out: "You there, with the legs! Are you a horse? I'm looking for a horse to be my friend."

The hen cackled, "Bad luck! Bad luck! Bad luck! I'm a hen, not a horse, can't you see?"

"But you've got legs!" said Brainbox.

"And I've got wings, too – look!" said the hen; and she stretched her wings and flapped them. "Hens have wings; horses haven't."

"No winged horses?"

"No. Hens, yes; horses, no."

"Pity," said Brainbox. To himself he thought: this question of wings or not-wings complicates everything. He decided not to think about wings or not-wings, but to concentrate only on legs.

Aloud, he said to the hen: "All the same, you could be a horse, couldn't you? You have legs."

"But only two," said the hen. "Hens have two legs; horses have four legs. Hens, two legs; horses, four legs. Hens, two; horses, four."

"So I need an animal with four legs if I want a horse to be my friend?" said Brainbox. He just wanted to check.

But the hen had seen a beetle in the grass. Without waiting to answer, she scuttled away after it, and Brainbox was left alone.

"Four legs . . ." he said to himself. He decided that he was sure he was right, even without the hen's saying so. "Four legs . . ." he repeated, memorizing the information. "Four legs . . . four legs . . ."

He began once more to trot down the lane.

The next animal he came upon was a dog who had just found an old bone. The dog was gnawing his bone, so Brainbox had time to look at him closely. Brainbox saw that the dog had legs. He counted them: one – two – three – four –

"I say!" he cried joyfully. "You've four legs – I've counted them! Exactly four! So, please – you are a horse, aren't you? I'm looking for a horse to be my friend."

The dog almost fell over with laughter; he even dropped his bone. Then he began barking madly at Brainbox: "Wruff! Wruff! Stuff and nonsense! Of course, I'm not a horse – I'm a dog – a dog – a dog!"

"But you've four legs," argued Brainbox. "Why shouldn't you be a horse?"

"My legs are dogs' legs," said the dog. "Quite different from horses' legs. For one thing, dogs' legs end in paws – look, like mine! Horses' legs end in hoofs, like yours. Legs with hoofs, that's what you want." And the dog picked up his bone and went off elsewhere to gnaw it undisturbed.

"I'm getting a more exact picture," said Brainbox to himself. "I must find a creature with legs, four of them, and hoofs at the end of the legs. Then I've found a horse to be my friend."

And he trotted off down the lane.

Further down the lane he met a sheep who was wandering up it, browsing on the wayside grasses as it went. When the sheep heard the horse coming, it lifted its head to stare.

"Legs," said Brainbox to himself. "And one – two – three – four of them. And each ends in – yes, in a little hoof!" He said aloud to the sheep: "Please, tell me: aren't you a horse?

You've legs – four of them – and four hoofs as well. Surely you're a horse? I want to find a horse to be my friend."

The sheep stared and stared. Then it said: "Baaaa! Baaaarmy – that's what you are! I'm a sheep; not a horse!"

"But your legs have hoofs!"

"Not like a horse's hoofs. Look at my hoofs – "

"I did," said Brainbox, "when I counted your legs."

"Now look at your own hoofs."

"Why should I look at my own hoofs?"

"You're a horse, aren't you?" said the sheep.

"What's that got to do with it?" said Brainbox, confused.

The sheep stared and stared. It bleated something to itself which Brainbox did not catch. Then it said: "A sheep's hoofs are cloven. A horse's aren't." And the sheep turned its back on Brainbox and began browsing again.

"Well," said Brainbox, trying to cheer himself up, "I'm getting nearer all the time. Legs; four of them; hoofs at the end of the legs; hoofs not cloven. Find all that, and I've found a horse to be my friend."

And he trotted off down the lane.

Further down the lane he met a donkey. They looked at each other. The horse saw that the donkey had legs. He counted them: one – two – three – four. He looked at the end of each leg: a hoof. He looked at the hoofs: uncloven.

Then Brainbox shouted at the donkey. "At last! You're a horse! And I've been looking for a horse to be my friend."

"Eeeyore! You're a fool!" said the donkey. "I'm a donkey, not a horse."

"But you have everything," Brainbox insisted. "Legs, four of them; hoofs, uncloven. *Why* aren't you a horse?"

"I've told you," said the donkey. "Because I'm a donkey."

Brainbox could have cried with disappointment. He stood, baffled and woebegone, in the middle of the lane, his head drooping almost to the ground in his despair. He did not know what to do next.

In the end, he begged the donkey to listen to the sad story of his search and advise him, and the donkey agreed. Then Brainbox told him all about his meeting with the snake and the hen and the dog and the sheep, and their helpful remarks. "So you see," said Brainbox, "I thought I could *work out* what a horse would look like. At least, I'd got the legs right."

"There's a lot more to a horse than a set of legs," said the donkey.

"I daresay," said Brainbox; "but I don't know any more. It all comes back to the fact that I've quite forgotten what other horses look like. I've got nothing to go on."

"You've something to go on," said the donkey. "You are a horse."

"Someone else said that to me," said Brainbox, puzzled. "They seemed to think it made a difference in some way."

"It does," said the donkey. "You know what another horse will look like."

"What will it look like?"

"Like you."

Brainbox was thunderstruck. "Like me . . ." He turned the idea over in his mind: it was new; it had possibilities; it might work.

"For instance," said the donkey, "look at your tail. Then look at mine."

Brainbox looked over his shoulder at his tail, and swished it. He looked at it carefully, as he had never bothered to do before, and saw that his tail was made up of a great number of very long, strong hairs. Then he looked at the donkey's tail: it looked rather like an old-fashioned bell-pull, with just a tuft of hairs at the end.

"Yes," said Brainbox, "I can see that our tails are quite different." He looked at the rest of the donkey, and then at as much of himself as he could see. He said, "I don't look very much like you at all, except perhaps for the legs."

"It's not just looks either," said the donkey. "A horse will have a special voice, just like your voice; and he'll have a special horse-smell, just like yours; and – and – well, when you meet another horse, you'll *know* he's a horse just because you're a horse, too."

"And you think I really might meet another horse?"

"I do," said the donkey.

"Then I'd best be off again," said Brainbox. "Thank you very much indeed for your advice." And he began trotting down the lane, in the direction from which the donkey had just come.

"Eeeyore!" the donkey called after him. "You're going to be lucky!"

Brainbox wondered what the donkey meant.

At the end of the lane, Brainbox came to a five-barred gate. A creature stood on the other side of the gate, with its head hanging over the top bar, looking sad. Brainbox saw that the creature was four-legged, with uncloven hoofs and a tail of long, strong hairs. But it wasn't just the creature's looks that excited Brainbox. The creature's smell was pleasantly familiar; and just when Brainbox was wondering what the voice would sound like, the creature lifted his head, looked straight at Brainbox, and said: "Neigh! neigh! The name's Dobbin. What's yours?"

"Brainbox," said Brainbox. "I'm a horse; and I *know* you're a horse, too. Why do you look so miserable?"

Dobbin said: "I live alone in this meadow, and I feel very lonely sometimes. There's no other horse to be my friend."

"Wait there!" said Brainbox. He turned round and began to trot back up the lane, the way he had come. The

donkey, who saw him approaching, called out, "You're going in the wrong direction!"

"No, I'm not," said Brainbox. "You wait and see."

He trotted on past the donkey and then past the sheep and past the dog and past the hen and past the grass-snake. They all stopped what they were doing to stare, when they heard the sound of horse's hoofs approaching.

When he judged that he had gone far enough, Brainbox turned and began to trot back towards the five-barred gate at the end of the lane.

He trotted faster and faster –

    past the grass-snake,

    past the hen –

– faster and faster, until he was cantering –

    past the dog,

    past the sheep –

– faster and faster, until he was galloping –

    past the donkey, who shouted "Hooray!" –

    – galloping – galloping – galloping –

till he came to the gate with Dobbin leaning over it –

"Mind out!" shouted Brainbox; and Dobbin drew to one side and Brainbox JUMPED. He went sailing over the five-barred gate, into the meadow.

"I've come to live here," said Brainbox to Dobbin. "To be your friend."

"Good," said Dobbin. "Very good indeed." He kicked up his heels for joy, and so did Brainbox. Then they galloped round the meadow together. When they were tired, they settled down to standing side by side, head to tail. Brainbox swished his tail to stop the flies from settling on Dobbin's head, and Dobbin swished his tail to stop the flies from settling on Brainbox's.

The two friends lived together in their meadow, keeping each other company, for many, many years. They were happy horses.

THE MOUSE AND THE SUN

A Canadian story

This is a story from the time long before the white men came to Canada. In those days, the animals ruled the earth. Alone on the great plains lived a little boy and his sister. Their father and mother had died when they were young. They had no uncles, no aunts, no grandmothers, no grandfathers; and so they were left to look after themselves. They lived many miles from other people. In fact, they'd never seen other people, only their parents.

The boy was very small. The girl was big and strong, and she had to find food for both of them, and do all the work in the house. She took her little brother with her wherever she went, so that he came to no harm. And she made him a bow and arrows to play with.

One day – it was winter – she went out to gather wood for the fire as usual, and took her little brother with her. He grew tired, and she told him to hide while she went further on in her search for wood. "Soon," she said, "you'll see a flock of snow birds flying overhead. Fire one of your arrows and bring a snow bird home for food."

The boy hid among the great hills of snow and watched the sky. He heard the sound of the snow birds' wings before he saw them. He fitted an arrow to his bow and fired – and another – and another. But his aim was poor, and he hit none of them. When his sister came back, bent double under her load of wood, he was ashamed to have to tell her that there was no bird for their supper. But his sister said: "Never mind. You'll get better at it. Tomorrow will be your lucky day!"

But tomorrow, when they went again searching for wood and again the little boy was left to watch for the snow birds – tomorrow didn't seem to be his lucky day. He shot and shot and shot again, but the birds flew past with a great rustle of wings. But then, at last, one snow bird fell out of the sky. He was very happy. Now he had something to show to his sister. "I shall try to kill one every day, for our supper," he said. "And you must skin them, sister, and when we have enough skins, I shall make myself a coat from them." And every day after that he went with his sister and waited for the snow birds to fly past, and every day he shot one down and took it home. And they skinned the birds and dried the skins. Soon there were enough skins for a coat. It didn't take many – he was a very small boy.

One day – proudly wearing his coat – he asked his sister: "Are we all alone in the world? Are there no other people?" Well, she said, she'd heard from their mother that other people lived far away to the east, beyond the mists of the prairie: and others, the people from whom their mother came, lived far away to the west, beyond the great hills. The little boy said: "One day, I'd like to see my mother's people!" So, when next his sister was away, hunting, he put on his bird-skin coat and took his bow and arrows and set out towards the distant hills to see if he could find his mother's people.

It was springtime. The sun had melted the snow; little streams were flowing, and blades of grass had begun to show above the ground. But the earth was soft and wet, and the day was hot, and warm winds blew. The boy walked on and on, and by the time the sun was high in the sky, he was very tired. He came to a little rise in the ground and lay down behind it, out of the wind. In no time he was fast asleep. And the sun beat down on him. It was so hot it singed his bird-skin coat, and the coat shrank and shrank until it was only a small patch on his back. And when he woke up and yawned and stretched himself, the coat burst – under his arms, across his back – it had grown so tight. He was very angry. The sun had ruined his beloved coat! He shook his fist at the sun and cried: "I'll have my revenge on you! You needn't think you're too high up there for me to get at you! Just you wait!" Without his coat he could hardly continue his journey, so he returned home.

For weeks he could scarcely eat. He talked about nothing but how the sun had spoilt his coat, and how he'd have his revenge. His sister tried to comfort him. Next winter, she said, when the snow birds came flying this way again, he could kill more of them, and she'd make him another coat. She'd make him two coats, or three! But he was not to be comforted.

At last he asked his sister to make him a snare, such as you catch rabbits in – but this must be a big one, for he meant to use it to trap the sun. She made him a snare from a strip of the skin of a buffalo, but he said it wouldn't do. It wasn't strong enough. So she cut off some of her long black hair, and made a snare from that. The boy said it would do

very well. And off he set, to catch the sun.

It was another long journey. But at last he came to the Great Water in the East. It was summer, and the sun rose early. The boy placed his snare where the sun would strike the land as it rose out of the sea, and then he went away and waited. Sure enough, in the morning as the sun rose burning out of the sea, it was caught in the snare and held fast. It could not rise; it was bound to the earth. "I told you!" cried the boy. "I warned you! *That's* for ruining my bird-skin coat." And he made the long journey home again.

And that day there was no light on the earth. Everywhere it was a sort of evening, more dark than light. The animals were terrified. The birds all fled to their nests, and only the owl came out to look for food. But then as the half-darkness went on, and on, they decided they must have a great meeting to discuss what to do. So all the animals gathered together. One of the birds, a goose, that had been bold enough to fly close to the sun where it struggled in the snare, was able to tell the rest of the animals what had happened. The sun was tied to the earth!

Unless they could free it, there would never again be real daylight. Someone, they decided, must go close enough to the burning sun to cut the cord that held it. It would be dangerous work, for the heat was tremendous: anyone who tried to cut the cord might well be burned to death.

They drew lots to see who should go. The lot fell to the woodpecker. So the woodpecker flew to the edge of the Great Sea, where the sun was trapped, and flew closer, and closer – oh, the heat of it! – till he was close enough to peck at the snare with his beak. Alas, alas, being a strand of woman's hair, it was very strong. He picked at it and picked at it, but it would not break. At last his head was so badly burned that he had to give up. His whole head was red from the great heat. And ever since then, the woodpecker in Canada has had a red head, where the sun singed him as the bird struggled to set it free.

Then the animals called for a volunteer to try to cut the snare. Now, at the time, the largest and strongest animal in the world was the mouse. The mouse was king of all the beasts, an enormous creature. It was his duty, he thought, to attempt that hard and dangerous task. So off he went: reaching the Great Sea in no time, so long were his legs, so fast could he run.

Once there, he attacked the snare with his teeth. But he could not bite it through. The heat was terrible. He would have run away, but kept telling himself that he *was* the biggest and strongest animal of them all: if he ran away, the smaller animals would laugh at him. So he went on, desperately using his great sharp teeth. While his back burned, and scorched, and smoked, he cut through one hair at a time. He began to melt away: the whole top of his body was burned to ash. But still he bit, and bit, and bit at that terribly strong hair. One hair after another parted. He was close to the end of his task and his whole body was melting, but now he came to the last hair of all. The hair parted and the sun rose free and sailed, as usual, high into the sky. It was day again. There was light again. The animals whistled, and cheeped, and grunted, and trumpeted with joy. And they made ready to welcome the mouse on his return from that brave adventure.

And here he came! Not, now, the largest animal in the world; now, almost the smallest. He was a hundred times smaller than when he set out. And his back was burned to ash. And ever since then, the mouse has been one of the smallest animals in the world; and his coat has always been the colour of grey ash, from the scorching he had when he freed the sun from a snare, long ago.

THE MUSICIANS OF BREMEN

The Brothers Grimm

There was once a donkey. He wasn't young, for he'd spent much of his life working for a farmer. He'd plodded and carried, as donkeys do. He'd taken sacks of corn to the mill, and sacks of flour back to the farm. And he'd never complained! But the day came when his old bones would carry no more sacks. He hoped he would be able to spend his last years quietly and comfortably in some corner of the farm. But the farmer was not a good man.

"Ah," he said. "So you can't work any more, eh? More than one sack and you're on your knees! Well, an old donkey is an idle donkey, and an idle donkey is no good to me. So . . . off you go! You can find your own way in the world now!"

And off the poor donkey trotted, out through the farmyard gate and into the road. There he stopped, and asked himself what he should do now.

"What *can* I do?" he thought. "I've never learned to do anything but carry sacks of corn and sacks of flour for that miserable, ungrateful farmer. All I'm good for now is eating and drinking and thinking about the good days when I was young." And he was so unhappy that he brayed, loudly.

And then an idea struck him.

"Wait a minute!" he thought. "Let me try that again!" And again he brayed, but this time more quietly. "Hmm!" he thought. "That's music! I've never thought of it before!

It's rather a nice sound!" And he brayed again, this time not loud, but not quiet, either. "I'm a musician!" he cried. "Yes, that's a very fine sound!" And he began to make his way slowly down the road, trying out his voice.

"Well," he cried. "That's a problem solved! Now I know what to do. I'll become a musician. I'll go to the nearest city – that's Bremen – I went there once or twice with my master. Yes, yes, yes, that's what I'll do!"

And off he trotted, practising his music as he went. He'd gone about a mile when he saw a dog lying by the roadside. The dog had the saddest look about him.

"Ah, hallo, dog," said the donkey. "What are you looking so miserable about?" And the dog howled.

"Oh, I'm old," he cried. "I'm old and I can't hunt any more. I can't smell things properly, you see. And I can't run too well. So my master's driven me away. After all the years I've hunted for him – *and* looked after his house at night! How I'm going to keep alive I don't know. I never could do anything but hunt – and look after houses – and bury bones." And he howled again.

"Hmm, cheer up," said the donkey. "I think I know the answer to your problem. Do that again."

"Do what?" said the dog.

"Make that noise you made," said the donkey.

"What, this?" said the dog, and he howled.

"Fine!" said the donkey. "A most interesting sound! You're a musician too, you know!"

"A musician?" said the dog, and he barked with surprise.

"Ah, that's even better," said the donkey. "I can see you've got more than one piece of music in you. You know, you're a very *clever* musician! Look, this is my plan! I'm going to Bremen to make my living as a singer. You come

along with me and – why, we could sing duets. We'll be the talk of the town!"

The dog growled. "Oh, all right," he said. "It sounds better than just lying here." And off they went together, practising their music as they went.

They'd gone another mile or so when they came across a very unhappy-looking cat. The cat was sitting by the road, too sad, it seemed, even to clean itself. It was rather dusty, and there was a dead leaf hanging from one whisker.

"Oh hallo, cat," said the donkey. "What are you looking so dismal about?"

The cat miaowed, sadly. "Oh, I'm old," she said. "I'm old and there's no edge to my teeth any more. And even if there were, my sight's that bad that I can't tell a mouse from a . . . mowing-machine. Haven't caught one for a whole year. Haven't even seen one for six months! So my mistress has driven me away. After all the mice I caught for her when I was young! And the games I played with her children, and the way I kept her lap warm in the winter evenings! How I'm going to earn my living, I don't know. I can't do anything but drink milk and sit snoring by the fire." And she miaowed again, most miserably.

"Hmm, cheer up," said the donkey. "I think I know the answer to your problem. Do that again."

"Do what?" asked the cat.

"Make that noise you made."

"What, this?" asked the cat. And she miaowed. It was a sound that would have broken your heart.

"Splendid!" cried the donkey. "That will bring tears to the eyes of the people of Bremen! A lovely sound, isn't it?"

And the cat miaowed again, and listened to the sound

she made. "Well, yes," she said. "I hadn't thought about it. It *is* rather lovely, I suppose."

"No supposing about it," said the donkey. "I could listen to it all day. Very charming! Cat, you're a musician too!"

"A musician?" cried the cat. And this time she purred, with pleasure.

"Oh, listen to *that!*" cried the donkey. "What superb singing! How do you manage so many different notes? Isn't it superb, dog?"

"Most superb, donkey," said the dog.

And the donkey explained their plan – to go to Bremen and make their living as musicians. "Why," he said, "if you come along with us, cat, we could sing trios!"

The cat miaowed and said, "Oh, very well. It will be better than just lying around trying to smell mice that aren't there."

So off they went together, practising their music.

They'd gone another mile or so when they saw on a gatepost a cockerel with his feathers drooping miserably. His fine red comb was flopping about his head in the unhappiest way.

"Ah, hallo, cockerel," said the donkey. "What are you looking so dreary about?"

The cockerel crowed – a very cracked sort of crow.

"Oh, I'm old," he said. "My happy days in the farmyard are over. My mistress is going to wring my neck and have me for dinner tomorrow. After all the times I've crowed in the morning to tell her it's time to wake up! Better than a clock I've been to her, and all she can think of is to wring my neck! Would you be happy if all you had to look forward to was being eaten? I don't know what I shall do. All I can do is crow." And he crowed again.

"Hmm, cheer up," said the donkey. "I think I know the answer to your problem. Do that again."

"Do what?" said the cockerel.

"Make that noise you made."

"What, this?" And the cockerel crowed.

"Magnificent," cried the donkey. "Isn't it a wonderful sound?"

"Most wonderful!" cried the dog and the cat together.

"You have great talent, my friend," said the donkey. "You see, you're a musician, too."

"A musician?" cried the cockerel. And he was so astonished that he crowed again.

"Oh, that *wonderful* sound!" cried the donkey. And he explained their plan – to make their way to Bremen and earn their living as musicians. "Why," he said. "If you come too, cockerel, we could sing quartets!"

The cockerel crowed, thought, and then crowed again.

"Oh, all right," he said. "It's better than being roasted and eaten, anyway."

So off they went together, the donkey, the dog, the cat and the cockerel, practising their music as they went.

But it was a long road to Bremen, and there was still far to go when night began to fall. The road ran into a forest, and it was black under the trees, and a cold wind blew. They decided they must rest for the night. So the donkey lay under a tall tree, the dog lay beside him, the cat climbed up among the branches, saying it was safer there, and the cockerel flew to the very top of the tree, saying he wouldn't feel safe any lower down.

In fact, the cockerel was so nervous that before he settled

he looked this way, and that way, and in front of him, and behind him, to make sure all was well. To the north there was nothing but blackness to be seen, and the same to the east and west. But when he looked to the south, there, not far away, was a small, warm light.

"I see a light!" he called. "A friendly-looking light!"

"That means a house," cried the donkey. "Well, if it's not far as a donkey walks . . ."

". . . or a dog . . ." said the dog.

". . . or a cat . . ." said the cat.

"Then we'll go," said the donkey. "We could do with something to eat."

"And somewhere comfortable to sleep," said the dog.

"And a nice warm fire," said the cat.

So they gave up the idea of sleeping in the forest and set off towards the light the cockerel had seen. Soon they came to a clearing, and in it was a small cottage, with a light shining out of its window. The animals crept out of the trees, and into the garden of the cottage. The donkey, being the tallest, gently laid his front hooves on the windowsill and peeped inside.

"What can you see?" asked the cockerel.

"Hmm. Food," said the donkey, "heaps of food!"

"Hurrah," said the cat.

"And drink! Plenty to drink!"

"Fine," said the dog.

"All set on a table, ready to eat."

"Good, good!" cried the cockerel.

"And more in the oven, by the looks of it!"

"I can't wait," cried the cat.

"And a nice warm fire!"

"Wonderful!" said the dog.

"And round the table, eating and drinking . . ."

"A kind old lady, who likes giving milk to cats?" said the cat, eagerly.

"And a kind old man, who loves giving bones to dogs?" said the dog, his mouth watering.

"They love animals – especially cockerels," said the cockerel.

"And they love music, too," said the cat.

"Let's go in," said the dog.

"No, no, you're all quite wrong!" said the donkey. "It's a band of robbers having their dinner!"

"Oh, *robbers!*" said the others.

"I don't fancy that," said the dog.

"Not my idea of nice people at all," said the cat.

"Well, that's that. Back to the forest," said the cockerel.

"I could almost taste that bone," said the dog.

"I could feel the milk going down, rich and creamy," said the cat.

"What I was thinking of," said the cockerel, "was corn. Rather a lot of corn . . ."

"Wait a minute!" said the donkey. He got down from the windowsill. "Wait a minute! I've got a plan. Now, listen!"

And, there in the cottage garden, they put their heads

together, and the donkey told them his plan. It was all they could do not to bark, and miaow, and crow, and bray with delight. It was a fine plan! They got ready to carry it out.

First the donkey got up on his hindlegs again and planted his front hooves on the windowsill. Then, very carefully, the dog climbed up on the donkey's back. The cat, with a silent spring, leapt up on to the dog's shoulders. And the cock flew up with the very quietest flutter of his wings and perched on the cat's head.

Now they were ready. At a signal from the donkey, they all began to sing. It was a mixture of braying, and howling, and barking, and miaowing, and purring, and crowing. It made a startling noise. The robbers in the room leapt to their feet, wondering what on earth was happening. Their wicked faces turned pale. And at that moment the donkey pushed open the window and the four musicians leapt into the room. And there was a tremendous sound of braying, and howling, and barking, and miaowing, and purring, and crowing, and crying and shrieking from the robbers.

Well. Even if you're a hardened robber you don't stay in a room at night-time when a strange noise outside the window has been followed by something with wings and hooves and several tails leaping through the window,

braying and howling and barking and miaowing and purring and crowing all at once.

In short, leaving their dinner on the table, the robbers ran away.

The musicians were delighted. "Hurrah!" cried the donkey. "Food! Bones!" cried the dog. "Drink! Milk!" cried the cat. "Comfort! And corn!" cried the cockerel. "Hmm, carrots!" cried the donkey. "I smell fish!" cried the cat.

"Let's eat!" said the donkey.

And eat they did – everything they could find, until they wanted nothing more but a long comfortable night's sleep. So out went the light, and the donkey lay down on a pile of straw, and the dog stretched out on a mat by the back door, and the cat curled up in front of the fire, and the cockerel flew up on the roof and perched there very happily, and they all went to sleep and dreamed of food and music.

BUT . . .

The robbers had not gone far. They were among the trees close to the cottage, watching and listening and plotting and whispering. And when the light went out, and everything became quiet, one of them went to find out what was going on.

He crept through the garden gate, up the garden path, through the front door, and into the room. It was completely dark. He groped for a candle. There was one on the table. He looked round for something to light it with. In the hearth he saw something bright and shining. The dying embers of the fire, he thought. So he bent down and blew to kindle the embers. To his horror the embers sprang at him and scratched his face. For, as you will have guessed, they were really the cat's eyes shining in the dark.

And now the robber crept no more. He ran as hard as he

could straight for the back door, and tripped over something. It bit him in the leg, and it barked. Then he ran twice as fast, into the yard, and there something gave him a kick behind, and it brayed. And the robber yelled, and that woke up the cockerel, and he stood there on the roof and shook his feathers and began to crow.

And the robber didn't stop running until he'd reached the rest of the robber band.

"There's a witch sleeping on the hearth," he cried, "and she jumped up and scratched my face! Oh, I wouldn't go back there for worlds! And there's a man with a knife by the door and he stabbed me in the leg! Oh, not for a fortune would I go back! And there's a great monster in the yard, and he beat me with a club! You'll never see me in that cottage again! And on the roof there's a devil, and he stood up and he shouted, 'Robber Doodle, Robber Doodle, shoo!' So I ran away, I can tell you that, I ran away as fast as my feet would take me, and if you've any sense you'll do the same. Run!"

And that's what they did. Off they ran, and they never came back.

As for the four musicians, they never got to Bremen, so we've no idea how well they would have got on with their music. The cottage was so comfortable that they decided to stay there and make it their home. And there was no one to drive them away, or to complain because they couldn't carry sacks of corn, or hunt, or catch mice, and no one threatened to roast them for dinner.

By the way, they do sing sometimes in the long winter evenings, for their own enjoyment. They bray, and bark, and howl, and miaow, and purr, and crow, and it's all very wonderful.

THINGS
ARE
PUZZLING

James Reeves

Alittle girl was walking along a footpath through a field, when she happened to meet an elephant.

"What is your name?" asked the elephant.

"Cristina," said the little girl.

"You are very small," said the elephant.

"Yes, I am a small little girl."

"Goodbye," said the elephant.

The next thing Cristina happened to meet was a mouse.

"What are you?" asked the mouse.

"I am a small little girl," said Cristina.

"You are very big," said the mouse.

"Goodbye," said Cristina, as she walked on.

The next thing she happened to meet was a giraffe.

"Hallo," said the giraffe. "What are you?"

"I am a big small little girl," said Cristina.

"You are very short," said the giraffe, bending his neck down so as to look at her closer.

Cristina said goodbye and walked on. The next thing she happened to meet on the smooth footpath was a very round and prickly hedgehog.

He stopped and looked up at Cristina.

"What are you?" he asked.

"I am a short big small little girl."

"You are very tall," said the hedgehog decidedly and trotted off before Cristina could say goodbye.

The next animal she happened to meet was a snake. She was not at all frightened, because she had never seen a snake before. But it ought to be mentioned that it is wise to be frightened of snakes until you have been introduced.

"What are you?" asked the snake.

"I am a tall short big small little girl," answered Cristina.

"You are very fat," said the snake.

"Goodbye," said Cristina, as the snake rippled off amongst the grass.

The next animal she happened to meet was a pig – a huge overgrown pig, grunting loudly.

"What are you?" he asked.

"I am a fat tall short big small little girl."

"You are *very* thin," said the pig, grunting.

"Goodbye," said Cristina.

The next animal she saw was a bird. It skimmed out of the sky and perched on a branch over the footpath.

"What are you?" asked the bird.

"I am a thin fat tall short big small little girl," answered

Cristina, who was beginning to get tired of being so many different things.

"Well, you are very slow," said the bird, chirping. "While you have been walking across this small field, I have flown three times round the world."

But he was lying. He had only been round it once.

"Goodbye," said Cristina, leaving the bird to rest on the branch.

The next animal she happened to meet was a tortoise.

"What are you?" asked the tortoise, rather out of breath from trying to hurry.

"I am a slow thin fat tall short big small little girl. *And* I know what you're going to say next. You are going to say that I am very quick."

"I wasn't," said the tortoise decidedly in his dry, scratchy voice. "I forget *what* I was going to say. You have put it out of my head."

"Well, perhaps you can tell me," Cristina went on, "why it is that I am called so many different things."

"Things are very puzzling," answered the tortoise. "It depends how you *feel*, not what people say. Take me, for instance. They call me slow, but I often feel quite quick. When I go for a walk with my grandfather, who is a hundred and seventy-three years old, he says I am far too quick for him. Goodbye for now."

Cristina decided to go home and have tea. That at least was not puzzling.

THE CHATTERBOX

A traditional Russian tale

There were once a man and his wife who lived in the middle of a village, in a pretty little cottage near the church. He was called John and she was called Mary. They hadn't been married long. They were very happy.

Well, the cottage made them happy. It was John's grandfather who'd planted the roses along the fence. And it was his great-grandfather who'd made the little front gate, where John and Mary stood in the evenings to watch their neighbours go by.

And it was their neighbours who made them happy. They'd known them all their lives. Standing by the front gate as the sun went down, they'd say, "Evening, Sarah! Evening, Tom! Evening, old Mrs Twistle! Evening, parson!"

And on Sundays they'd all go to church together, and it would be, "Morning, Sarah! Morning, John! Morning, Mary! Morning, old Mrs Twistle! Morning, parson!"

And John's work made them happy. He worked down on the great farm, that was owned by the lord of the place. He was a great lord indeed.

Everybody liked John and Mary. "Ah, they're a nice couple," people would say. "He's as nice as his old father was." "Ay, and *his* father before him." "And she's a good kind woman." "And her mother was a good kind woman, too." "Ay, and *her* mother before her." And so on.

BUT . . .

Though everyone thought Mary was a good kind woman – and she *was* – everyone also thought she was a chatterbox. She was a gossip. She was a tittle-tattle. You couldn't trust her with a secret.

So young Mrs Twistle, who was old Mrs Twistle's son's wife, would say, "Do you know what? My daughter Susan's thinking of getting married. You'll never guess who she's going to marry, Mary."

"Oh," Mary would say. "It must be that young man I've seen her with from the village the other side of the forest. Tom Trott – is that his name?"

"The very one," young Mrs Twistle would say. "She likes him and he likes her. And the long and short of it is they mean to get married in the spring. But it's a secret, Mary. They don't want anyone to know until Christmas. Young Tom wants to tell everybody at Christmas. You won't say a word to a soul, will you, Mary?"

And Mary would say of course not, she wouldn't say a word to anyone. The secret was safe with her. And she always meant it! Only . . . well, it was so exciting to have something secret to tell. And she'd meet Jenny Thrush, who was married to Jim Thrush, and she'd say, "Yes, my dear – married in the spring, she'll be, to that young fellow from the village on the other side of the forest. Tom Trott, that's his name." And then she'd remember her promise. "Oh dear," she'd say.

But by then it was too late.

So John and Mary were very happy, and all the time everybody liked John, and most of the time everybody liked Mary.

BUT . . .

Well, one evening, after work was over, John went into the forest. There were wolves about in those times, and John had found one of their dens, and he went along to dig it out. But he hadn't dug more than a foot into the ground when there was a *clink*. And another *clink*. And another . . .

Round things that went *clink*!

John picked one up and gave it a bit of a rub. My goodness! It was gold! It was treasure! It was a great heap of gold coins that someone had buried!

"Oh," thought John. "Now Mary and I can buy our own cow – and a bit of land of our own!" The ground was still going *clink* as he dug at it. "And I could buy Mary some pretty dresses!" *Clink, clink!* "But, of course, I'll have to keep it quiet. That lord of ours – if he got to hear of it, he'd want the gold for himself. He's got gold of his own, but he's a greedy man. We'll have to keep it quiet – both of us. Me and . . . Mary . . . Oh dear, oh dear! *Mary!* She'd never keep exciting news like this to herself."

What was he to do?

He was such a lucky man, he thought, but such an unlucky man too. Married to Mary, who was good and kind, and whom he loved. But a chatterbox!

He'd dug up all the coins now – there were hundreds of them – and then he'd buried them again. But how could he go home and tell Mary? She'd be bound to tell the next person she met. And that person would tell another person, and the lord would get to hear of it.

But then John had an idea!

He started on his way back home, and anybody who'd been watching would have been puzzled. Because John was dancing. He was dancing with delight. Because it was a wonderful idea he'd had!

Soon he came to the river. The day before he'd set a fish-net in the water. Now, when he pulled it out, he found a fine fish caught in it. So he took it out and off he went again.

A little further along, near the edge of the forest, he'd set a trap. There was a hare caught in it. He took out the hare and put the fish in the trap. Then he hurried back to the river and put the hare in the fish-net.

Then, still dancing with delight, he set off home. He went down the village street. "Evening, Sarah! Evening, Tom! Evening, old Mrs Twistle! Evening, parson!" And into his little cottage, where Mary was waiting for him.

"Oh, John, dear," she cried. "I wondered where you were – it's getting dark!"

"Mary, my love," said John. "I want you to do something for me. I want you to heat up the oven and then bake me as many pancakes as you can."

"John, my dear husband!" cried Mary. "Whoever heard of anyone heating up the oven at this time of day! And who'd want to eat pancakes at bedtime! Even one pancake – let alone as many as I could bake!"

"Mary, my love," said John. "Don't argue! Oh, how can I tell you my news? The fact is we're rich! We're rich!"

"John! Dear John!" cried Mary.

"It's all right, my love," said John. "It's true! Digging in the forest I found a heap of gold . . ."

"Oh, John!"

"And we must bring it home in the darkness, so no one will see what we've got. Oh, Mary, my love, don't argue! It's gold! So warm the oven and bake the pancakes!"

"Gold! Oh, John! Oh, John! You shall have as many pancakes as you can eat, dear husband. No wonder you are hungry! Finding gold . . . !"

"That makes you hungry, Mary my love," said John.

And together they cried, *"Finding gold makes you hungry!"* And then they laughed with excitement.

So Mary warmed the oven and baked the pancakes.

Though she was laughing so much she could hardly remember what she was doing.

"Here's the first lot, John, my dear," she said. "Eat them while they're hot, and I'll make some more."

And she was so excited that she didn't notice that John ate only one of the pancakes. The rest he slipped into his sack.

Soon she was back with more pancakes. Was that enough? Could they go and get the treasure now?

Not yet, said John, not yet. They mustn't go out and into the forest until the whole village was asleep.

So she made more pancakes, and still more. And every time John ate one, and slipped the rest into his sack. She couldn't make them fast enough. Ah, said John. It was a long way to go to where he'd buried the treasure, and the gold would be heavy to carry. He must give himself strength. More pancakes! And still more pancakes!

And at last his stomach was full, though his sack was even fuller. And off they set into the night.

John went first with his sack. Mary came after, trying not to laugh with excitement. She wanted to go and tell the whole world about the treasure John had found! She thought of all the dresses she'd buy: especially one she'd seen when the pedlar came round in the spring. It had ribbons! And she'd buy new shirts for John: especially some beautiful white ones for Sundays. She was so busy thinking of all this that she didn't notice what John was doing ahead of her in the darkness. He was feeling in his sack and taking out a pancake and slipping it over the branch of a tree. First one, and then another. A pancake on this branch, a pancake on that branch. Mary was thinking how they'd have a new chair made for old Mrs Twistle, when she suddenly caught sight of the pancakes.

"Growing on the trees!" she cried. "Pancakes! John, John! Have you ever seen that before?"

"What's that, my dear?" said John.

"There are pancakes growing on the trees," said Mary.

"Oh, they're not growing there, my love," said John. "Whoever heard of pancakes growing on trees! Didn't you see that great cloud of pancakes that went over some minutes ago?"

"A cloud of pancakes?"

"It was a very big one. It rained pancakes very hard for a moment. You must have been dreaming if you didn't notice."

"Oh, that's true, dear John," said Mary. "I was thinking what we'd do with our treasure!"

"Ah, Mary," said John, "what we'll do with our treasure! Yes! Well, we're nearly there. But . . . look! There's a trap I set not far from here, for a hare. Let's go and see what we've caught. Won't take a minute."

They left the path and made their way under the trees to where John had set his trap. "Here it is!" he cried. "Oh, Mary! How lucky we are! There's a fine fish in here!"

"A fish?" said Mary. "A fish in a trap you set for a hare? But how could a fish get into such a trap? We're nowhere near the river yet, John."

"Sssh, Mary, my love," said John. "Don't get excited! Even here, someone might hear us! Didn't you know there are fish that can walk?"

"Oh, I'd never have believed it," said Mary. "Fish that can walk! Well, well!"

And soon they could hear water. They were near the river. John said, "I've a net somewhere here. Let's stop for a moment and see if we've caught anything in that." They made their way under the trees to the river bank. "Ah," cried John. "Here it is! And my goodness – a hare! A fine fat hare caught in my net! That's a good thing, my dear! We may have found gold, but we'll still be glad of a fine hare for Sunday dinner, won't we?"

"But what is the world coming to?" said Mary. "A hare in a fish-net? A hare in the river? How can that be?"

"Mary, my dear," said John. "You're the sweetest of wives, but you know very little of the world. You've never seen pancakes in trees, you've never heard of a walking fish, and now you've never heard of a water-hare!"

"A water-hare?" said Mary. "Is that what it is?"

"Of course it is," said John. "Well, on we go."

And at last they came to a tree with a scratch on it. John had marked it so he would be able to find the gold. And he took his spade, and dug – and there was the treasure. And he filled his sack with the gold – there was plenty of room, now the pancakes were gone.

And then, as happy as two people ever were, they made their way home.

Well, yes, they were happy. But in the darkness, poor Mary jumped at every sound. They were nearly home and passing near the lord's great house when they heard the bleating of his sheep.

"Oh, John," cried Mary. "Dear John! What's that? What's that terrible noise?"

"Run, dear Mary!" cried John. "Run for your life! It's the little bad creatures that live in the forest. They must have got into our lord's house and are pinching him black and blue, poor man! Run!"

And they ran and they ran until they reached the village. They ran up the street, past the church, into their cottage. They stowed the bag of gold under the bed. Then they leapt into bed themselves, and were soon fast asleep. That is after John had sleepily said, "Remember, my love, not a word to a soul about our treasure!"

And Mary had sleepily replied, "Of course, dear husband. I wouldn't dream of saying a word to anyone!"

And Mary meant it! Not a word would she say! Not even to her dearest friend! Especially not to her dearest friend, who lived in the cottage across the street! Especially not to her dearest friend, to whom she always told everything!

Though nothing she'd ever told her dearest friend had been half as exciting as what she now had to . . . What she now had *not* to tell!

NOT to tell!

NOT to tell!

Not even to her dearest friend!

Next morning, she was across the road and sitting in her dearest friend's kitchen. "Such news," she was saying. (And she was yawning! Well, it *had* been a late night!) "But I can't tell you anything about it!"

"You're very tired this morning, Mary!" said her dearest friend.

"So would you be if you'd been up half the . . . Oh!" said Mary.

"Up half the night, you mean?" asked her friend. "Oh, Mary, what *is* it?"

"Oh, it's such a vexation that I can't tell you," said Mary. "And it isn't as if it's every day one's husband digs up a great heap of gold!"

"Gold!"

"Oh, oh," said Mary. "What have I said?"

What *had* she said! To her dearest friend – who was soon speaking to *her* dearest friend – who spoke to old Mrs Twistle – who spoke to the blacksmith – who spoke to his wife – who spoke to her married daughter – who told her husband – who told the shepherd – who spoke to old Mr Twistle – who'd already heard it from his wife *and* from Mary – who'd also told the forester's wife – who'd told the parson's wife – who'd told the parson . . . And the parson had told the lord himself, up at the great house.

"What's that!" the lord cried. "Have them sent here, man and wife! We'll get to the bottom of this! Treasure found in the forest is *my* treasure! Have them brought at once! I've never heard of such a thing!"

He said a lot more, and all of it angry. Any gold found in those parts was *his* gold! "*Grrrh!*" he said, and his face was red with anger.

And so, up to the great house went John and his trembling wife. And the lord began shouting again.

"How dare you!" he roared. "How dare you keep gold found in the forest to yourself! I'll have you whipped! I'll have you turned out of your cottage! I'll have you – oh, nothing's bad enough for you." He glared at John. "Well, man – say something!"

"My lord," said John, "what is there for me to say, except that I know nothing of any treasure? It's some strange mistake . . . some . . ."

"Don't try to deceive me!" cried the lord. "It's useless to deny it! Everyone in the village knows about it. And how do they know about it? Because your wife here told them about it!"

"My wife!" cried John. "My dear wife! Ah, my lord, now I understand. She's a good woman – ask anyone in the village – and I love her dearly. But, my lord, there's no believing a thing she says. She's . . . Er . . ." He went closer to the lord and spoke in a whisper. "She's rather silly, my lord. She imagines things. She's . . . ah . . . a little . . . ah . . . you understand me, my lord?"

"I understand that you're an impudent fellow," said the lord. "Do you think you can get away with a story like that? Now, hold your tongue while I speak to your wife. If I'm not mistaken, I'll soon get the truth from her!" He turned to Mary. "Now, tell me, good woman, did your husband not find a treasure?"

"Oh yes, my lord," said Mary, who was still trembling. "Indeed he did."

"And where did he find it?"

"In the forest, my lord."

"Ah, and you went to fetch it?"

"Yes, at night, my lord."

"At night? Why at night?"

"Because, my lord, my dear John said – oh dear – "

"What did he say?"

"He said if you knew of it you'd take it from us!"

The lord roared like an elephant.

"Ah, the truth!" he cried. "I knew we'd get it. Take your time, woman, and tell the whole story. Tell me what happened, step by step."

"Well, my lord," said Mary, "we went into the forest, and – it was the night it rained pancakes."

"The night it did what?"

"I thought the pancakes were growing on the trees, my lord! What a silly woman I was! I didn't notice the cloud of pancakes as it passed overhead."

"You didn't notice the . . . ! What happened then?"

"Oh, after that we looked in one of my husband's traps, my lord, and there was a fish in it."

"There was a *what?*"

"It was silly, my lord – I mean, I was silly. Can you believe it, but I didn't know that fish could walk. At least, as your lordship will know, not being a silly woman, *some* fish can walk."

"Some fish can – *what?*" The lord growled like a dog.

"You'll not believe it, but I was even surprised when we came to the river and found a hare in my husband's fish-net."

The lord couldn't speak. His face was becoming redder and redder.

Mary laughed. "It was a water-hare, of course," she said. "Can you believe it, my lord – I didn't even know there were hares that lived in the river." She laughed even louder. "And I didn't even know about the bad little creatures that come out of the forest and pinch your lordship black and blue in the night. We heard them, it was horrible, as we came home. And that reminds me, your lordship – I should have asked you before – how *is* your lordship? Not too badly hurt, I hope? I just hope they don't come and pinch you every night!"

The lord spluttered.

"Oh," said Mary, "I've forgotten the most important thing, my lord. After we'd found the hare in the river, we found the gold. It was in a hole in the ground, and – "

"Don't tell me any more," said the lord. "There were lots and lots of gold pieces . . ."

"Oh yes, my lord," said Mary.

"And you picked them up and took them home."

"Oh yes, my lord."

"Oh, don't tell me any more," said the lord. Even his ears were red with rage. "I'm not a fool, you know. Your story is worthless, woman. You're a silly creature. I'm sorry for your husband. Off with you both, before I lose my temper!" (If he hadn't lost his temper already, John thought, why were his ears so red?) "And let no one bring me any more ridiculous stories about finding gold told by silly women."

"You see, my lord," said John. "It's as I said. You can't believe a word that passes her lips. But she is a dear kind soul, for all that."

Mary never did understand what had happened. I think some of their friends in the village began to understand, when they thought it over. And they probably smiled to themselves. Well, you were always sure of a good meal or something good to drink if you visited John and Mary in their cottage. They seemed to live very comfortably. Mary had some very nice dresses, and no one had whiter shirts on Sundays than John.

And everyone thought Mary was very good. And very kind. And a good wife to John. It was just that . . .

Well, as old Mrs Twistle said, she was a gossip, and a tittle-tattle – and a *chatterbox*.

THE PRINCE WHO HAD DONKEY'S EARS

Retold by Edward Blishen

Once there were a king and a queen and their newborn baby son. He was a prince, of course. And there were three fairies, who'd come with gifts for the baby.

The first fairy smiled beautifully and said: "No prince in the whole world will be more handsome!"

And the second fairy smiled even more beautifully and said: "No prince in the whole world will be wiser or more honest."

The third fairy smiled only a very small smile. She was worried. The handsomest prince in the world! The wisest prince in the world! The most honest prince in the world! Wouldn't that make him the proudest prince in the world? Wouldn't he grow up thinking there was no one like him? Wouldn't he grow up too proud by half?

She thought, and she thought, and then she said: "My gift is that he shall have . . . donkey's ears. Very big, very pointed, very hairy donkey's ears. And that will prevent him from being too proud."

You can imagine how anxious the king and queen were. They watched the young prince grow more and more handsome. They watched him grow more and more wise, and more and more honest. But they also watched his ears

233

grow huger and huger, and hairier and hairier, and more and more pointed. No doubt about it, those were donkey's ears!

Well, they didn't want anyone to know about *that*. So they let his hair grow. It grew to his shoulders, and no one would have known that he had ears at all. But then it went on growing. The time came when the prince's hair simply had to be trimmed.

But the barber who cut his hair was sure to find out about those dreadful ears! What was to be done?

What the king and queen did was to send for the best barber in the land. He was to trim the prince's hair, they said, once a week. He would be wonderfully well paid for it. But in doing it he would discover . . . something rather surprising. And about that he must say nothing. If he told anyone at all what he had seen, he would be punished with death.

The barber wondered what he would find under the prince's hair. But of course he couldn't say no to the king

and queen. And for a barber it was the best job in the
kingdom. Even the king didn't have a barber who lived in
the palace, was paid in gold, and ate royal food at the royal
table. The barber was happy.

That's to say, he was happy until he trimmed the prince's
hair for the first time. Then, at once, he found those
terrible ears. He was so shocked that he dropped his
scissors. The prince said sadly:

"I know you have promised the king and queen that you
will keep this secret to yourself." And the barber nodded
and picked up his scissors and went on trimming the
prince's hair.

But oh, that secret! It is a terrible thing to have such a
secret to keep. The barber longed to tell someone else,
anyone at all. He didn't want people to laugh at the prince.
He just wanted to share the secret. Well, you know how
having a secret makes you long to give it away.

So the barber was well paid and well fed but he was
unhappy. And then he remembered that living in a forest
near the palace was an old man known to be extremely wise.
So the barber slipped out and visited him. He didn't tell the

wise man what the secret was. He simply said he had one, an awful one, and longed to tell it. What could he do?

Well, said the wise man, there *was* an answer to that. The barber should find some place as lonely as possible. There he should dig a hole. Then he should tell his secret to the hole, and fill it in again.

"The ground," said the wise man, "will never give you away. You will have told your secret and only the earth will know of it."

So that's what the barber did. He went to the loneliest place he knew, he dug a hole, and he told his secret to the hole. And my goodness, how cheerful he suddenly felt! He filled the hole in again, and he sang all the way back to the palace. That surely was the end of his troubles!

But it wasn't.

Out of the earth where the barber had dug his hole, some stout reeds grew. Now, they were just the sort of reeds for making whistles. Along came two shepherds, cut two reeds, and made two whistles. And then they played them.

But these weren't at all like ordinary whistles. They didn't play the tunes the shepherds wanted to play. Instead, out of both came a thin whistling voice that sang, again and again:

> "The prince has donkey's ears,
> Did you know?
> The prince has donkey's ears . . .
> Did you know?"

Well, soon everyone knew. The shepherds told their friends, and their friends told *their* friends, and from friend to friend it passed until the king heard of it. He had the shepherds brought to him, and ordered them to play. Oh, they tried so hard to make the whistles play some other tune! But all that came out from both, in that thin whistling voice, was the song that now the whole kingdom knew:

> "The prince has donkey's ears,
> Did you know?
> The prince has donkey's ears . . .
> Did you know?"

Imagine the king's anger! He knew who must have given the secret away. It could only be the barber. He ordered the poor man to be brought to him at once. He had been warned! If he told anyone about the prince's ears, he would die. And the king called for the executioner.

But at that moment the prince stepped forward.

"Father, *father!*" he cried. "Why should the barber be punished for telling the truth? It is true, I *have* donkey's ears! But what does the shape of my ears matter? I'd rather have ordinary ears, of course. But, I suppose, if they're good enough for an honest donkey, they're good enough for an honest prince."

And with his hands he swept his hair back so everyone could see his ears. And they all gasped.

They gasped and they turned pale. And then they began to cheer.

"But," they cried, "your ears are just like anybody else's!"

And so they were. Because there had been a part of the fairy's gift that she had kept to herself. It was that if ever the prince showed that he wasn't proud, that there was no danger of his being the proudest prince in the world, then his ears would become ordinary ears.

And so everybody was happy. I think you can guess who was the happiest of all. It was the barber, of course. If the prince hadn't lost his donkey's ears, the barber would have lost his barber's head.

But what about the whistles, you ask? Well, there was a naughty child or two who tried them out, in the hope of hearing that thin whistling voice crying:

> The prince has donkey's ears,
> Did you know?

But now that everyone knew, and anyway the prince had ears like anyone else, the song was never heard again.

HOW THE FROG FROM OSAKA MET THE FROG FROM KYOTO

A Japanese tale

This is the tale of two Japanese frogs. One lived in a rather small pond in the city of Osaka, which is by the sea. The other lived in a rather narrow ditch in the city of Kyoto, which is not by the sea. They were both perfectly happy, except for one thing. The frog living in Osaka was always wondering what the city of Kyoto was like. And every now and then the frog living in Kyoto would say to himself, "I wonder what sort of place Osaka is?"

One day, and it happened to be the same day, neither of them could bear it any more. The frog in Osaka woke and thought, "I *must* make the journey to Kyoto!" And the frog in Kyoto woke and thought, "I *must* make the journey to Osaka!" And they both sighed. Well, one was very comfortable in his rather small pond, and the other was thoroughly at home in his rather narrow ditch. But how could you live in Osaka all your life and never know what it was like in Kyoto? And how could you live all your life in Kyoto and never know what it was like in Osaka!

So off they went, on their long hopping journeys. They hopped for dusty mile after dusty mile. They hopped along sunny lanes. They hopped across rice-fields. Suddenly it rained all over Japan, and they hopped through thousands of puddles. They hopped through villages. And at the very same moment when the frog from Osaka came to the foot of

a high hill, the frog from Kyoto also came to the foot of a high hill. As a matter of fact, it was the same hill, but of course, one was on the side nearest to Osaka, and the other was on the side nearest to Kyoto. And hopping rather wearily, each climbed to the top.

And there they met.

Imagine that! They stretched themselves under a tree with their legs spread comfortably behind them. Oh, how nice to have a rest from all that hopping! And, of course, they talked.

"I'm from Osaka," said the frog from Osaka. "I live in a rather small pond, but if ever you find yourself in that part of the world, you'd be very welcome to stay. Plenty of flies, and rather nice muddy water. Oh, I wouldn't mind being back there!" And as he thought of his pond, and his friends, and all that marvellous mud, his huge bright frog's eyes filled with tears.

"And I'm from Kyoto," said the frog from Kyoto. He stretched his weary legs and sighed. "I live in a rather

narrow ditch, but if ever you visit the city, do come and spend a day or two with me. We've lots of flies, too, and some particularly muddy mud. Oh, I do wish I was home again!" And as he thought of his ditch, and his friends, and that particularly muddy mud, there were tears in his beautiful green and yellow eyes.

"May I ask why you've left home?" said the frog from Osaka.

"Oh, I thought I must go and see the city of Osaka," said the frog from Kyoto. "But what are you doing on the top of this hill?"

"Oh, I couldn't be happy until I'd had a look at the city of Kyoto," said the frog from Osaka.

Well, you can imagine their surprise! Fancy a frog from Osaka, going to Kyoto, meeting a frog from Kyoto, going to Osaka! And on top of a hill!

"Oh, what a pity!" said the frog from Kyoto. "If you think of it, being on the top of a hill, I ought to be able to see Osaka from here. And you ought to be able to see Kyoto. In the distance, of course. Very far away. Looking very small. But we could see enough to decide if it was worth going on. But we're not tall enough."

"It's the trouble with being a frog," said the frog from Osaka. "Don't get me wrong. I like being a frog."

"It's a good thing, being a frog," said the frog from Kyoto.

"But," said the frog from Osaka, "we're not tall enough to see things in the distance."

"Wait a minute," said the frog from Kyoto. "Tell me what you think about this. Suppose we stand up, leaning against each other . . ."

"Balancing on our back legs," said the frog from Osaka.

"Holding on to each other's front legs."

"So we don't fall over."

"Then I could look at Osaka! Over there in the distance!"

"And I," said the frog from Osaka, "could look at Kyoto, somewhere in the distance over there!"

"Shall we try it?" asked the frog from Kyoto.

"Let's try it," said the frog from Osaka.

So they tried it. *Very* carefully. First they moved as close as they could. Then they raised themselves on their strong back legs, their hopping legs. Then they leaned against each other, one set of front legs braced against the other. And it worked! Suddenly, instead of being two frogs flat on the ground, they were two tall frogs standing, able to see into the distance.

So they looked.

The frog from Osaka looked, as he thought, at the city of Kyoto. And the frog from Kyoto, as he thought, looked at the city of Osaka. And both of them croaked with dismay.

"Oh, how disappointing!" cried the frog from Osaka.

"Oh, what a disappointment!" cried the frog from Kyoto.

"What can you see?" asked the frog from Osaka.

"I see Osaka," said the frog from Kyoto. "But it's exactly the same as Kyoto. And what do you see?"

"I see Kyoto," said the frog from Osaka. "But it's exactly the same as Osaka."

And so they let themselves down on to the ground again. And they lay there sighing. All that hopping, through all those lanes, and puddles, and villages, and rice-fields! And Kyoto turned out to be exactly like Osaka, and Osaka

turned out to be exactly like Kyoto.

"Well, I'm not going any further," said the frog from Osaka. "I'm going back to my pond."

"And I'm not going any further," said the frog from Kyoto. "I'm going back to my ditch."

And so, as well as frogs could, they bowed to each other. Well, you know how the Japanese always bow when they meet and when they part. In this respect, Japanese frogs are just like Japanese people. And then they turned and went home – the frog from Osaka, of course, to Osaka, and the frog from Kyoto, of course, to Kyoto.

Now, I'm not going to say frogs are stupid. They are not. But those two frogs had forgotten something. They'd forgotten they were different from other animals not only in not being tall. Frogs, you remember, have their eyes at the top of their heads. And so, when they stood balanced against each other –

Do you see what I mean?

The frog from Osaka was looking backwards at Osaka. No wonder he thought it looked just like Osaka – it *was* Osaka. And the frog from Kyoto was looking backwards at Kyoto. No wonder he thought it looked just like Kyoto – it *was* Kyoto.

I must say they were glad to get back to their friends, and the flies they were fond of eating, and their marvellous muddy mud. But from that time on, if you asked the frog from Osaka about Kyoto, he'd grumble, "Not worth a visit! It's so like Osaka, you can't tell the difference!"

And ask the frog from Kyoto about Osaka, and he'd croak, "Don't go there! All they've done is copy Kyoto."

And as he hopped away you'd sometimes hear him grumble, "Copycats!"

THE TORTOISE, THE MONKEY AND THE BANANA TREE

A tale from the Philippines

Once upon a time a tortoise was sunbathing by a river. You might think a tortoise, with its thick shell, couldn't sunbathe. But you'd be wrong. The warmth comes up from the ground and, of course, the tortoise sticks its head out, and as much of its neck as it can. It's soon very warm indeed.

Well, this tortoise was almost asleep when she noticed a tree being carried downstream. And no ordinary tree, either. It was a banana-tree. She dived in, swam to the tree and began pushing it towards the bank. But a banana-tree is a very big tree: and though this was a fair-sized tortoise, she couldn't pull it up the bank. The tree still had its roots and leaves, and they were heavy with water.

So the tortoise did the sensible thing – she ran for help. That's to say, she ran as a tortoise runs: a fairly slow business. But not far along the road she came across her neighbour, the monkey.

"I say! Come and look!" said the tortoise. "I've found a banana-tree. Help me carry it to my garden so I can plant it there!"

The monkey thought for a moment, as monkeys do, and then he said:

"Right you are! But only if you agree that we share the tree."

Of course, said the tortoise. So they went to the river and, working together, just about managed to tug the tree up the bank and then drag it to the tortoise's garden. And the tortoise said, "Right. Now we'll dig a hole and plant it."

But the monkey thought for a moment, as monkeys do, and said, "You agreed we should share the tree, and I'm against planting it."

The tortoise said, "Of course we'll plant it. Then we'll wait till bananas grow on it, and we'll share them. What else could be done with it?"

"What else?" said the monkey. "Well, to begin with, we could divide it up at once: half for you, half for me. That's

much better than hanging around waiting for bananas to grow on it."

The tortoise grumbled, but the monkey said he wouldn't agree to anything else, so the tree had to be sawn in two.

The monkey looked at the two halves, and decided the top of the tree looked the nicer half – much greener, not those dirty roots! – so he said, "I'll have the top half!"

And he seized the top of the tree, dragged it away to his garden next door and planted it there. The tortoise was left with the bottom half of the trunk and the roots. This she planted with great care, pressing the earth down all round, and watering it with can after can of water. While she did this, the tortoise was thinking; because tortoises think, just as monkeys do – but sometimes it's a better sort of thinking. Anyway, a slow smile began to spread across the tortoise's small leathery face. And then she prepared to wait.

In the monkey's garden next door, the green top part of the banana-tree soon turned brown and the leaves dried and fell off. The tree began to lean sadly to one side, and soon it was dead. But the bottom half of the tree, in the tortoise's garden, put forth new leaves, and then flowers, and then bananas. They call the clumps of bananas, because of the way they grow, hands. Well, this tree was crowded with hands of ripening fruit.

And the smile on the tortoise's leather face grew larger and larger, until –

Until she began to wonder how she was going to pick the bananas.

I'm sure you see the problem. Tortoises, as is well known, cannot climb trees. From the beginning of time to the present moment, no tortoise has ever climbed a tree. And I very much doubt if a tortoise ever will.

The tortoise thought and thought, and as she did so her smile changed to a frown, and her frown to a glare. She thought again, trying to think better thoughts than her first thoughts; but there was no way out of it. She knew only one creature able to climb the tree and pick the fruit, and that was her neighbour, the monkey.

So she put on the best face she could and went to visit him.

"Well, I'll pick the fruit for you," said the monkey, "but –"

"But what?" asked the tortoise, nervously.

"But I'll want half the bananas for my trouble," said the monkey.

Well, as they say, beggars can't be choosers; so the tortoise had to agree. And grinning broadly, the monkey shinned up the tree and, reaching the top, calmly began to eat the bananas. Not one did he throw down to the waiting

tortoise. "Hi!" cried the tortoise. "Half for you – half for me! Remember? So every time you eat one, throw one down to me."

But the monkey only laughed – the sort of laugh you get from a monkey when its mouth is full of delicious ripe bananas. "No," he said. "No! These are awfully good bananas, by the way. You must have looked after them very well! – No! You cheated me when we divided the tree. You let me take the worthless half, though I'm sure you knew it wouldn't grow. So now I'm going to eat every single banana!" And it began to rain banana skins as the monkey tossed them down from his perch at the top of the tree.

If tortoises could turn purple with rage, that tortoise would have turned purple with rage. As it was, she did some thinking; and then she crawled off to the other end of the garden and gathered some blackthorn branches. These she scattered on the ground under the tree. Then she hid.

The monkey came to the end of his feast and, very much

heavier than when he went up, leapt down from the tree. He landed right in the middle of the thorns. "Ow!" he cried. "Ouch! Ow!" And he leapt from foot to foot, and shrieked and screeched. The tortoise, watching from where she lay hidden, smiled and then laughed and, if a tortoise could have split her sides, she'd have split her sides.

Which was the worst thing she could have done. That's to say, to laugh. For the monkey now knew where she was hidden, and he ran there and while she was helpless with laughter, picked her up and turned her on her back. And, as you know, a tortoise on her back is a useless tortoise. A tortoise on her back doesn't know how to get on to her front again.

"And now to punish you!" cried the monkey. "I'm not sure what's bad enough for you. Shall I beat you with a stick? No, that would be too kind! Shall I put you in a mortar, as if you were grain, and pound you to pieces? No, that would be too gentle!" He was still picking thorns out of his toes, and growing angrier and angrier. "I think throwing you off the top of a very high mountain might be about right!"

But the tortoise had been doing some upside-down thinking, and she said, "Oh dear, do whatever you like with me: beat me with a stick, pound me to pieces in a mortar, throw me from the top of the highest mountain in the land: I don't mind, as long as you don't throw me in the water! Oh please, *don't* throw me in the water!"

"Ho ho!" cried the monkey. "So that's what you're most afraid of! Right! Into the water you shall go!"

And he picked up the tortoise, carried her to the river and threw her in. Splash! To the monkey's great delight, the tortoise disappeared under the water. "That's the end of

252

you," he cried.

But at that very moment, here came the tortoise's head, above the water; and she was smiling. Then, with quick little movements of her legs, off she swam. And to the frowning monkey, the smiling tortoise said, "Thank you, you extremely foolish creature! I'd have thought even you would have known that water is my second home!"

And within a minute or so, or not much longer, she was out of sight.

Acknowledgements

For permission to reproduce the copyright material acknowledgement and thanks are due to the following:

Harper Collins Ltd for "The Witch and the Little Village Bus"; Canongate Publishing Ltd for "Beautiful Catharinella" from *Grimms' Other Tales*, translated by Ruth Michaelis-Jena; Edward Blishen for "The Toymaker's Shop" by Marie Smith; J M Dent and Sons Ltd for "Don't Cut the Lawn!" from *The Downhill Crocodile Whizz and Other Stories* by Margaret Mahy; Puffin Books for "The Steadfast Tin Soldier" from *Hans Andersen's Fairy Tales* retold by Naomi Lewis (Puffin Books 1981 © Naomi Lewis 1981); David Higham Associates Ltd for "The Sea-Baby" from *Eleanor Farjeon's Book of Stories, Verses and Plays* by Eleanor Farjeon; Diana Denney for "Prickety Prackety" by Diana Ross from *The Tooter* published by Faber & Faber Ltd; David L. Harrison for "The Giant Who Threw Tantrums" from *The Book of Giant Stories* by David L. Harrison; David Higham Associates Ltd for "Rabbit and the Wolves" from *Tortoise Tales* by Ruth Manning-Sanders; Jonathan Cape Ltd and the estate of Arthur Ransome for "The Tale of the Silver Saucer and the Transparent Apple" from *Old Peter's Russian Tales* by Arthur Ransome, illustrated by Faith Jacques; Faber & Faber Ltd for "The Fairy Ship" by Alison Uttley from *John Barleycorn*; Little, Brown & Co for "The Cat and the Parrot" from *Tales Told in India* by Virginia Haviland; Harper Collins Ltd for "The Mermaid's Crown" by Ruth Ainsworth; L. Pollinger and Farrar, Straus & Giroux, Inc for "Why Noah Chose the Dove" by Isaac Bashevis Singer; Laura Cecil for "Brainbox" from *The Lion at School and Other Stories* by Philippa Pearce (© Philippa Pearce 1971); Blackie and Son Ltd for "Things are Puzzling" from *Egg-Time Stories* by James Reeves.